DAT¯ ¯

Fl

Boothill Town

BOOTHILL TOWN

Leslie Scott

THORNDIKE
CHIVERS

This Large Print edition is published by Thorndike Press®, Waterville, Maine USA and by BBC Audiobooks, Ltd, Bath, England.

Published in 2004 by arrangement with Golden West Literary Agency.

Published in 2004 in the U.K. by arrangement with Golden West Literary Agency.

U.S. Hardcover 0-7862-6218-4 (Western)
U.K. Hardcover 0-7540-9939-3 (Chivers Large Print)
U.K. Softcover 0-7540-9940-7 (Camden Large Print)

The text of this Large Print edition is unabridged.
Other aspects of the book may vary from the original edition.

Set in 16 pt. Plantin by Liana M. Walker.

Printed in the United States on permanent paper.

British Library Cataloguing-in-Publication Data available

Library of Congress Cataloging-in-Publication Data

Scott, Leslie, 1893–1975.
    Boothill town / by Leslie Scott.
      p. cm.
    ISBN 0-7862-6218-4 (lg. print : hc : alk. paper)
    1. Gold mines and mining — Fiction. 2. Prospecting — Fiction. 3. Large type books. I. Title.
PS3537.C9265B66 2003
  813'.52—dc22   2003067193

Boothill Town

CHAPTER 1

Two men stood in the vestibule of the Espantosa Hills and gazed north. *Espantosa,* in Spanish, means haunted, terrible, and those grim hills, in appearance at least, did not belie their name.

Andy Webb was old. He was short, stockily built, his untrimmed whiskers were grizzled, his faded blue eyes set in a network of wrinkles. But there was a twinkle in those faded eyes, and the litheness of his movements and the spring of his step said he had far from lost the vigour of his youth.

Mort Lane was young, tall, broad-shouldered. His unruly hair was black and he had steady grey eyes. His lean, bronzed cheeks were covered with a growth of black beard. He looked hard and fit, and he was.

Both men's clothes were patched and faded. Their boots were scuffed, their hats as disreputable as wind, rain and sun could make them. They looked the part of desert rats to perfection.

Webb was one, and had been for forty years. Mort Lane, ex-cowhand, was well on the way.

"Mort," old Andy said, "all we'll find in those blasted hills is a grave."

He wagged his grey head and frowned at the hills in question. He turned a disapproving gaze on his young partner, fished a hunk of eating tobacco from his pocket and worried off a chaw. His jaws worked ruminatively for a few minutes. He took careful aim and drowned a lizard six feet distant with a stream of amber juice. The lizard swam out, shook a browned and disgusted head and put another yard of distance between him and the prospector. Webb measured the distance with his eye and "pulled trigger" again. The lizard swam out a second time and went away from there.

Mort Lane chuckled, produced "the makings" from his shirt pocket and rolled a cigarette. Through the blue wisps of smoke he contemplated the hills for which they were heading.

It was not an enticing prospect. Brown, gaunt, strewn with boulders, slashed by canyons and wide dry washes, their rocky ridges standing out like the swollen veins on a dying man's forehead, they fanged upward to the hard blue of the Texas sky. They had a grim, forbidding look and were austerely uninviting. Cactus, greasewood, sage and mesquite struggled to survive on their stony slopes, and did so in scattered patches. But where a spring trickled forth from under a cliff or underground water fertilised the earth, the thickets were dense and stood out in black bristles against the brown monotony of the slopes.

Old Andy Webb didn't like the looks of those wide, dense thickets.

"This is Indian country," he remarked pessimistically. "Leastwise Indians have always passed through this way a lot, from down in the Big Bend country and around the Guadalupes."

"Get up to date, old-timer," scoffed Lane. "Indians are all on the reservations."

"Sounds good," Webb replied drily. "Only thing wrong with it is it ain't so. There are still plenty of bands sliding up from Mexico. Apaches and Comanches, and they're bad. They work through the mountains, sticking to hill country like this, and on north till they circle into New Mexico. Their route has always been right through here. Enough cover up there among those rocks to hide away a whole tribe. Uh-huh, all we're going to find up there, Mort, is a grave."

"We'll chance it," Lane returned lightly. "We came all this distance from the Big Bend for a look-see at this ground. No sense in backing out now. And I still believe we have a chance to hit it rich up there."

He fumbled several chunks of rock from his pocket as he spoke.

"Don't forget, these are from up there," he remarked significantly.

Andy Webb took the fragments and examined them with care, as if he had never seen them before. As a matter of fact, he had examined them a score of times with never failing interest and a trace of excitement.

"They're rich, all right," he admitted. "All shot and veined with wire gold. And you still believe that Mexican gambler's yarn that he got 'em up in the Espantosa Hills?"

"Don't see why he'd lie to me," Lane replied. "After all, I did him a mite of a favour."

"Just saved his worthless life, at the risk of your own, as I gather," Webb snorted. "But just the same maybe he lied about where he got the specimens, or was plumb loco. Why didn't he go back and look for the place where they come from himself?"

"Well, for one thing, he wasn't a prospector," Lane went over the ground covered a dozen times before in the endless argument. "He found the stuff but didn't understand what it meant. Before I took up with you, I wouldn't have understood its significance, either. Now I know, as does anybody who's done a mite of prospecting, that the rocks are washed down during rainy weather when the gullies are full of water, maybe from miles distant from where he found them. He just browsed around where he picked them up, didn't find anything else worth while and came away. He didn't have any supplies and was just passing through, not looking. Didn't try to trace them to their source. He said he did figure to go back for another look some day, but you seem to forget what I told you about him. A Texas Ranger all of a sudden showed up and sort of persuaded him to go back to McMullen County and have a little talk with a grand jury about a shooting over there. I've a notion that about now he's dressing awful loud, wearing his hair kind of short and staying indoors of nights."

"He'll live longer in the penitentiary than we're likely to in those hills," Webb declared, still pessimistic. He turned and gazed southward.

"Good prospecting country down there,"

11

he said. "I've always believed there's metal in those ridges."

"Maybe, but it wouldn't do you much good if you found it," Lane pointed out. "That's rangeland down there and over to the east and west, mostly privately owned. Nope, it's us for the hills."

"And a grave!" Webb growled. "Might as well expect to find metal in a grindstone as in those rocks up there. Prospectors have been passing these hills by for years."

"Yes," Lane retorted, "just as they passed by the Tombstone Hills over in Arizona. And then along came Ed Schiefflin and took millions in silver from them. And the gold miners in Nevada walked over the Comstock Lode that later made a score of men rich. And hundreds walked past the Mother Lode in California. What's been done once can be done again."

"Oh, well, come along," Webb sighed resignedly. "We can camp on that mesa up there ahead. There's a crick running across it and plenty of grass for the horses and mules."

The mesa was over three miles distant, with a fairly steep climb of several hundred feet to its level expanse. Flanking the southern base of the hills, it was a mile in depth and two miles wide. It was dotted with trees and clumps of thicket, mostly near the creek banks, and grass-grown. Over it loomed the sinister ramparts of the hills.

From its floor the view to the south was magnificent. Mile on mile of rolling rangeland, with a range of mountains pencilling a blue line along the distant horizon. East and west the hills curved around it, so that the little plateau lay like a lamb between the paws of a crouching lion.

The prospectors made their camp on the south bank of the creek. The bank was shelving, with a drop of about four feet to the water. To the east and west of the little clearing in which they built their fire was dense thicket which afforded a comfortable wind break. The thickets were less than a score of yards distant. They supplied plenty of dry wood, and the fire burned brightly, its smoke rising straight into the sky.

In the crystal-clear air, that column of smoke could be seen for miles. And it *was* seen.

Old Andy Webb surveyed the scene with the appreciation of a desert wanderer.

"Fine place to build a house," he remarked.

"Even finer to build a town," said Lane.

Webb snorted. "Prairie dog town!" he jeered. "Those varmints are the only things

13

would live out here miles from nowhere."

Mort Lane looked thoughtful. His grey eyes narrowed a trifle, and he pushed back his battered, broad-brimmed "J.B." and ruffled his thick black hair in a gesture habitual to him when pondering some notion. However, he said no more and watered Rojo, his big red sorrel, Webb's sturdy roan and the two pack mules. He hobbled the roan and the mules but let the well trained sorrel roam free, knowing he would not stray. Webb busied himself preparing the evening meal.

The sun was down when the partners finished eating. The sky above the western mountains was aflame with scarlet and with gold. The east was a timeless infinity of steel blue, shot and dappled with exquisite rose. To the south the more distant mountains were a violet shadow shaded with purple and mauve, save for one towering spire that caught the last sun rays and gleamed molten silver above its sombre base. And over the mesa hung the grim hills with their sparse thickets bristling up like the stiff beard on a scarred dead face and the rising wind moaning eerily against their crags and pinnacles.

Lane rolled a cigarette, cowboy fashion, with the slim fingers of his left hand. Webb fished out a black pipe and stuffed it with blacker tobacco. For some time they smoked in comfortable silence. Then they cleaned up and, after making sure the horses and the mules were comfortable, spread their blankets beside the dying fire to sleep the dreamless sleep of wasteland wanderers. And as they slept, a ring of death closed around them.

CHAPTER II

It was the warning snort of Rojo that awakened Mort Lane in the dead dark hour before the dawn. Instantly he was hair-trigger alert. He had learned to respect the reactions of the highly intelligent horse. Rojo didn't let loose that explosive blow for nothing. It meant that something had startled him, something of which he was not exactly sure. A moment later he whistled his breath softly through his nose. And Lane knew instantly that it was no prowling mountain lion or inquisitive coyote that had disturbed the sorrel. As he listened with straining ears, he heard a slight scuffling sound in the thicket to the west, such a sound as a carefully placed foot might make when slipping slightly on an unexpected round stone.

Lane reached out and touched Webb. Old Andy awoke without sound or movement. With the wariness of a seasoned campaigner, he did not start or speak out. His own fingers tapped the back of Lane's hand, and that was all.

"Something in the thicket over to the right," Lane breathed. "I don't like it, Andy."

"Indians!" Webb breathed back.

"Maybe," came the faint whisper in reply. "If it is, they're getting ready to rush us in the first light."

"They'll cut loose with their guns soon as they can see us," breathed Webb. "What are we going to do?"

"This," Lane replied. "Ease out of your blanket and leave it rolled where it is. I'm doing the same. Then crawl to the edge of the creek bank and slide over. Got your rifle? Okay. No noise or we're done."

The manoeuvre was executed success-fully and without the slightest sound. The partners crouched under the shelter of the slightly overhanging bank, peering in-tently toward the black mass of the thicket beyond the bedrolls beside the ashes of the dead fire. The night was very dark and ut-terly silent, but pregnant with menace. The clammy chill of the wan mist rising from the surface of the stream touched their faces with ghostly fingers as the black water slid noiselessly past. All nature seemed to be holding its breath in the presence of some stealthy terror.

There followed a long and trying wait, the most disagreeable part of a fight, in which a man grows nervous and begins to reflect earnestly upon his sins. Lane and Webb knew that if there were really Indians in the thicket and they meant business, they would not attack until just before the dawn in the common native fashion, thinking to surprise and rush their victims in the low and puzzling light. Also, the chances were that the savages were Apaches, and Apache gods forbade a night attack; the night was sacred to ancestral ghosts. They would wait and watch during the hours of darkness.

The east began to grey. The stars paled from gold to silver, dwindled to pinpoints of steel. A faint breeze shook down a myriad dew gems from the grassheads. Somewhere a bird sang a liquid note and was still. The silence again became intense as the wind lulled and the light steadily increased. Objects grew dimly visible.

With paralysing suddenness the silence was shattered to shards by a roar of gunfire. The blanket rolls beside the dead fire twitched and jerked as bullets hammered them. Echoing the reports came an appalling screech and a crackling of the brush. From the thicket burst five horrific figures, faces streaked with paint, low-slanted eagle feathers fluttering from dingy white turbans. Feet encased in high boot-moccasins thudded on the ground as the Apaches rushed the camp, knives gleaming in the dawn light.

Webb's Winchester boomed sullenly. Both Mort Lane's six-guns let go with a rattling crash.

Three Apaches went down before that blazing volley. The remaining two leaped high in the air with yells of consternation. Down they came and bounded forward like rubber balls. Again came a crash of gunfire from the creek bank, and a fourth savage fell, jerking and clawing on the very edge of the bank. The fifth, with a ululating howl, plunged over the crumbling lip and squarely on top of Mort Lane.

Down they went together in a kicking, slashing, striking tangle. One of Lane's guns was dashed from his hand. He pulled the trigger with the other and heard the hammer click on an empty shell. He lunged forward frantically with his empty hand, and by sheer luck his fingers coiled about a sinewy wrist and held. He lashed at the Indian with his empty Colt, but the savage writhed aside like a greased eel. Lane's wrist came down across his bony shoulder and the second gun went flying.

Over and over they rolled at the edge of the water, the Indian tearing and clawing at Lane's face with his taloned fingers. Lane struck out with all his strength, felt his fist connect with an impact that jarred his arm to the elbow. At the same instant he forced the knife-holding hand upward and back. They whirled over, the Apache underneath. The Indian let out a yell that ended in a bubbling shriek. He gave a hollow groan, flopped madly about, stiffened, relaxed, and was still. Lane staggered to his feet.

"Good Lord!" yelped old Andy. "You're covered with blood! Where'd he dig you?"

"No place," Lane panted, shaking himself disgustedly. "It's his blood, not mine. He fell on his own knife. Drove it clean through him. Are the rest of the hellions dead?"

"Sure look it," Webb replied, peering through the strengthening light at the stark forms scattered around the clearing. "Let's make certain."

"Careful!" Lane warned. "They're good at playing possum, and a wounded Apache is deadly as a broken-backed rattler."

However, the savage raiders were all satisfactorily dead.

"Mescalero Apaches, all right," said Webb. "Come up from Mexico on a raid.

20

They must have seen our smoke last night and figured there'd be some pickings here. That was a fool trick, building that big fire out in the open; I ought to have known better." He snorted and swore.

"What'd I tell you?" he demanded accusingly. "We ain't even in those hills yet, and we came within an inch of getting scalped!"

"But we weren't," Lane returned cheerfully. "Well, let's collect the carcasses and drop 'em in that crevice over there and cover 'em with rocks. Don't want to leave them lying around. Some more of the same sort might come along and find them, and then try to nose us out to even up the score."

"Chances are they'll do it anyhow," Webb predicted.

With considerable labour they disposed of the bodies, jamming them in the crevice and covering them with rocks and loose earth.

"Graves!" grumbled Webb, straightening his aching back. "Didn't I tell you? Started already. Graves!"

"We're not in 'em," Lane pointed out. "The omen is good."

"Just a little hint of what we got coming," retorted the pessimist. "Might as well put their rifles in the packs; they're good irons. Wonder where they stole 'em?"

21

Lane searched the thicket with his eyes. "Chances are there'll be some ponies over the other side of the brush," he remarked. "We'll round 'em up and drive them into the hills with us."

"That's your chore," said Webb. "You're the one who used to be a cowhand, before you took to looking for rocks."

"And graves," grinned Lane.

Old Andy swore and started building up the fire. Lane set out to round up the Indians' horses.

However, corralling the half-wild mustangs proved too much for even Mort Lane, former tophand on numerous spreads. Finally, in disgust, he drove them across the mesa and down its sloping side. He nodded with satisfaction as he watched them, tossing and snorting, vanish into the south.

"They'll head for the grasslands on the other side of the arid stretch," he told Webb. "We'll clean up, cook some breakfast and head into the hills."

After eating, they got the rigs on their horses and loaded the mules.

"Well, which way shall we go?" asked Lane.

"All directions are the same," growled Webb. "We might as well head east and work on around through the hills till we get back

22

where we started from. We ain't going to be stopping any place for long; that is, unless we stop somewhere for good, which is quite likely."

Lane chuckled. "Okay," he agreed, "to the east it is."

Prospecting is the most aggravating form of gambling the diabolic gods of chance ever invented to drive men insane. The history of mining is crammed with freakish happenings, some of them so outlandish as to challenge belief.

In California two pocket miners used to go to a neighbouring village in the afternoon and return by night with household supplies. Part of the distance they traversed by trail, and nearly always sat down to rest on a great boulder that lay beside the path. In the course of years they had worn the boulder tolerably smooth, sitting on it. Then one day two vagrant Mexicans came along and occupied the seat. They began to amuse themselves by chipping off flakes from the boulder with a hammer. They examined one of the flakes and found it rich with gold. The boulder paid them eight hundred dollars. But the most aggravating circumstance, from the viewpoint of the two miners, was that the Mexicans realised that there must be more gold where the boulder came from. So they went panning up the hill and found a pocket from which they took, in the course of three months, more than a hundred and twenty thousand dollars worth of gold.

Prospectors wandered over a certain section in Nevada for years, and found nothing. Then along came a man who built a cabin by a stream and started raising hogs. The hogs rooted about, turning over the earth in little piles. Rain washed the piles down, the lighter earth floating off, anything heavier settled to the ground. The hog raiser one day noticed something peculiar where his porkers had been rooting. He investigated, and from two pockets uncovered by the industrious pigs he removed five thousand and eight thousand dollars' worth of metal respectively.

Hank Williams, prospecting in the Tombstone Hills, was so disgusted with his luck that he resolved to head for home the following morning. That night his two mules broke loose and wandered off. Searching for the animals the next morning, Williams spied a gleam of metal in the trail left by the dragging halter chains. He investigated. The result was the Grand Central and Contention mines, the richest ever found in the section.

The stories of mischances, accidents, overlooked opportunities are legion.

Mort Lane and Andy Webb turned east instead of west, and turned their backs on a fortune!

CHAPTER III

During the days that followed, Lane began developing a disquieting feeling that the veteran prospector might be right in his contention that there was no metal to be found in the Espantosa Hills. Perhaps the Mexican wanderer had made a mistake and had confused another range of hills with the Espantosas. Be that as it may, if there was gold bearing ore in the hills, they were reluctant to give up their treasure.

"I tell you the rock ain't right," old Andy repeated over and over. "It ain't gold bearing rock. These formations ain't quartz; they're basalt — trap rock, spouted out by volcanoes millions of years back. And you don't find gold in trap rock. Yes, sir, that's all these hills are — trap rock. And what else? Snakes and cactus and lizards and sage and greasewood, that's all. Dry camps half the time at night, and dust and sun all day long. We've worked back almost to where we started and ain't found a thing, and ain't going to. Grub's getting low, too, and nothing to shoot 'cept varmints a buzzard wouldn't eat. Son, we're just chasing rainbows."

"I still believe we'll hit it," Lane declared stubbornly. "That Mexican who gave me the specimens described these hills to a T. He said he got the stuff here, and I believe him. We'll hit it."

Webb groaned and set about making camp.

That night, after old Andy was wrapped up in his blankets and snoring, Lane sat by the dying campfire thinking of the past two years and what had gone before.

Mort Lane had been born and brought up during the cow country's booming years, when the longhorns rolled northward in a steady stream. He had ridden with many a herd to cross the Canadian, the Red and the Cimarron and on to Abilene or Dodge City. Texas was rolling in prosperity that many thought would never cease.

And then the bubble burst and hard times came to the cattleland. Riding jobs were scarce. Old-timers held onto what they had and the younger men were cast adrift. Lane was finally reduced to chuck line riding — wandering from one spread to another in search of a meal, a night's lodging, and maybe a few days of work digging postholes, mending fences, breaking wild horses or other such menial tasks. At Marathon on the northern edge of the Big Bend country, he met old Andy Webb in a saloon. They got to talking about range conditions, prospecting, and so on. Finally Webb, who had taken a shine to the young cowboy, made him a proposition.

"Son," he said, "what say you throw in with me? I've been prospecting for forty years, and though I've never hit it rich, I've always been able to make a fair to middlin' good living. I'll grubstake you, and you can come along until things get better in the cow business."

Lane had ridden into Marathon with the clothes on his back, his two guns, his magnificent red sorrel horse and his saddle, and little else. What he would have laughed at a year earlier suddenly sounded attractive.

"Okay, old-timer, I'll give it a whirl," he said.

That was two years before, and during the course of those two years Mort Lane had learned to live a carefree, leisurely life under the sun and the stars.

They never made a rich strike, but they had made a living and were able to lay aside

28

a few dollars against a possible bad time. But Mort Lane, who dreamed of some day owning a cow spread of his own, still saw that day far in the future.

One day when rummaging in the bottom of his saddle pouches, he had unearthed the specimens of ore given him a few years before by a Mexican dealer he'd befriended in the course of a bar-room brawl. He had laughed over the incident at the time and had forgotten all about the bits of rock crisscrossed with wire gold, until he came across them in the pouch.

When he showed them to Webb, the old prospector was struck with the richness of the metal content; but when Lane told him where the Mexican had found them, Webb scoffed at the story.

"I know the section," he said. "No metal there. That oiler was just pulling your leg. Forget it!"

But Lane didn't forget it, and as they worked farther and farther north past the Apache Mountains, the Sierra Diablos, and the Delawares, he kept the matter in mind. And when they spent a few days in Buckley, just east of the Guadalupes, he remarked to Webb:

"Andy, folks here tell me the Espantosa Hills are only about forty miles to the north and a bit east. What say we give 'em a whirl?"

"Well, I reckon the only way to get that nonsense out of your head is to show you it's nonsense," Webb replied resignedly. "Okay, we'll go up there and get snake-bit or shot or die from drinking arsenic water or something. Okay!"

Recalling Andy's caustic comment, Lane chuckled and joined the old prospector in sleep.

The following morning they came to the mouth of a narrow canyon, the sides of which were perpendicular cliffs of dark rock. Its floor, which had a fairly steep upward slant, was scoured into ruts and gullies and littered with boulders and float.

"Well, guess we'd better have a look-see here," suggested Lane.

"Okay," agreed Webb. "Then we'll have covered every foot of this infernal country. But I tell you we're just wasting our time. Look at those cliffs; they're trap rock."

"Some of this float doesn't look like trap rock to me," Lane pointed out.

Webb grunted disgustedly, and they turned into the canyon, leading the horses, the mules ambling patiently in the rear.

"Lots of water comes down here in the rainy season," observed Lane.

"Uh-huh, and if we happen to get caught by a cloudburst in this crack, we'll be drowned before we dry out," Webb replied with his usual pessimism.

Lane nodded. "But look at the float scattered about," he said. "I've a notion those cliffs up ahead get all busted up in the spring thaws."

Webb was not enthusiastic. However, he industriously gathered and examined float from force of habit. They were some distance up the canyon when he suddenly uttered an exclamation.

Lane peered at the jagged fragment Webb held in a hand that shook a little. It was streaked and stained with mineral. He took it and went to work with a chipping hammer. The stone split at the first blow. Lane stared, and uttered a low whistle.

"Andy, look here," he said in a strained voice.

Webb stared, his eyes widening in disbelief. He glanced up at the dark cliffs.

"It ain't so," he muttered. "It can't be!"

"It is!" whooped Lane, fumbling in his pocket. He produced his specimens.

"Look!" he exclaimed. "Andy, they're the same. This must be where my *amigo* from *mañana* land picked them up. They're the same!"

"You're right about that," Webb conceded. "They're both wire gold. But how the devil and where the devil! Look at those cliffs! I tell you they're trap rock and not quartz."

"Then where did this stuff come from?" countered Lane.

"I don't know," Webb muttered. "Let's go see."

Walking so fast they were almost running, they continued up the canyon. The horses and mules were forced to trot to keep up with them. Old Andy said nothing, but Lane could see he was wild with excitement nevertheless.

Lane kept picking up more float, splitting it and exclaiming over it. Webb eyed the cliffs, a bewildered pucker between his brows. He kept shaking his grizzled head.

They were perhaps half a mile up the narrow gorge when the old prospector suddenly halted, staring upward. The ground at the base of the cliff was littered with huge fragments of stone. Its crest was cracked and ragged. A deep, wide gash extended some distance down the beetling wall.

"Son," old Andy said, his voice shaking, "son, I've got it. Look up there — where the rock has been knocked off by a lightning flash. *That's* not trap rock. *That's* quartz! I understand it now. The trap rock that faces the cliffs is in the nature of a casing. That's often, almost always, in fact, the way a metal-bearing ledge runs: metal-bearing ore veins between casings of base rock. Yes, I understand it now. Sometime, millions of years back, there was some sort of a great upheaval here. A split in the earth's surface formed this canyon. Or maybe there was a great slip caused by a fault deep down in the earth, causing a section of stone to slide over this way from perhaps miles distant. I lean to some convulsion that caused a split, however. This canyon is as if a great flaming sword had cut down through the earth, leaving a wound. And the 'sword cut' went through the trap rock and just missed the quartz ledge here to the north. I'll bet everything we find that there's nothing but trap rock to the south; but here to the north the trap is just a thin skin over the quartz. No prospector that knew a thing about the business would have even troubled to come up here after a glance at those trap rock cliffs. Just one of those freak things that makes prospecting interesting and prospectors go loco. Let's have a look at those big chunks over there."

They went to work with the chipping hammer and a sledge. They broke up fragment after fragment. Always it was the same: the rock was streaked and studded with metal.

"And sure to be high-grade pockets," Lane exulted.

"Wrong!" said the veteran. "It's *all high-grade!* And the veins must run for miles. Partner, we're rich!"

They followed the formation far up the canyon, and from occasional outcroppings, now apparent once they knew what to look for, Webb was convinced that the metal-bearing veins were of great extent.

"And there'll be offshoots and separate ledges," Webb said. "We can locate half a dozen claims if we're of a mind to."

"I'd say claims for each of us at what you consider the best ground should do," replied Lane. "Let other folks have the rest."

"Sounds right to me," conceded Webb.

Lane nodded. "But, Andy," he said, "we're locating *three* claims on the best ground."

"Three?"

"That's right. One for you, one for me, and one for my Mexican friend who first found the strike."

"That's a plumb fine notion," agreed Webb. "And from what I've seen, I'd say the very best ground is about where that lightning flash knocked down the rock. Close to the mesa, too, which is an advantage. I'll fill out the forms right now. Let's see, what is that jigger's name?"

Lane looked blank. "Darned if I know," he replied.

"Oh, well, it doesn't matter," said Webb. "Call him Pedro. All oilers are named Pedro or Juan. And Lopez is a good Mexican name, about as common in *mañana* land as Jones is up here. One claim for Pedro Lopez. You won't have any trouble nosing him out if he's over at the state prison for that shooting, as you figure. A hefty passel of *dinero* may help to get his sentence shortened."

"Wouldn't be surprised," Lane agreed. "As I gathered from the Ranger, it was a shooting over a monte game, not a snake-blooded killing. Chances are he didn't get an overly heavy sentence."

At the close of the day, old Andy was bubbling with enthusiasm.

"Mort," he said, "this is going to start a stampede that'll make '49 look like a Sunday school picnic. Just wait till we get to town and spread the news! The setting is perfect, too. Just a couple of miles to the mesa down there, and fairly easy going all the way. Won't take much road building.

35

And there's plenty of water on the mesa to operate the quartz mills. It's prime!"

Lane nodded thoughtfully, a contemplative expression in his grey eyes.

That night they camped on the mesa, with good water and plenty of wood for their fire. Lane managed to knock over several grouse in the thickets, and they feasted royally on the first fresh meat they'd had for a long time. Well fed and content, they talked over plans for the future.

"Well, we've located and posted our notices," Webb said. "The next thing is to head for town and file."

"Yes, we'll file our claims, but not right away," Lane replied slowly.

"Eh? Why not?"

"Because," Lane said even more slowly, his eyes looking out over the distances, "first we're going to get title to this mesa. It's all state land, Andy. We've got a few pesos salted away between us, and we can get this land for mighty little. We'll take measurements, run lines and put up posts. Then we'll get in touch with the Land Office and get title. There'll be nothing to it. Nobody wants this section, and nobody knows about the gold. We can acquire a nice holding for little or nothing."

"What the devil do we want with it?"

asked the bewildered Webb. "Ain't no gold ledges down here."

"That's where you're wrong," smiled his partner. "The biggest ledge of this whole section is down here, the one worth the most money."

Old Andy wagged his grizzled head. "Knowed it to happen before," he observed sadly to the nearest mule. "Hit on a prime metal strike and they crack up. Uh-huh, go plumb loco and begin imagining things. Didn't think it'd happen to him, though. Always seemed a level-headed younker; but you never can tell. Too bad!"

Mort Lane chuckled. "Don't you see it, old-timer?" he urged. "Don't you see that the real gold mine is down on this mesa? As you said, this strike is going to start a regular grass-fire stampede, just like the silver strike over at Tombstone did. And this is no pocket strike. The lodes in those cliffs are liable to keep on producing for years and years. What does that mean? It means that folks by the thousand will be pouring in here."

He paused to roll a cigarette, his eyes glowing, while old Andy stared at him open-mouthed.

"Folks have to eat and have to have places to live in," he resumed, warming to his subject. "Where there will be one miner swinging a pick, there'll be half a dozen other folks providing for his needs and helping him spend the money he makes. It will mean a town in this section, a hell-roaring town, and the only place for a town is on this mesa. And once it gets going, it'll be here to stay. Even if the gold peters out in a year, which I don't figure it will, the town will keep going. It won't be like the ghost towns up in Nevada and over in California, that closed up shop when the metal in the hills was gone. This is a perfect location for a convenient supply station for the south, the east, and the west. Look over there right now!"

He paused to point to where, only a few miles to the east, a swarthy dust cloud was rising into the darkening sky.

"Know what that is, Andy?" he continued. "That's dust kicked up by a trail herd rolling north to the railroad over the Coronado Trail. They're pushing 'em hard, trying to get to water and good grass as soon as possible. All the herds from the south, east and west use the Coronado through this section, and it's a hard drive. If there was a town here, the herds would lay over to rest the cows and give the hands a chance for a mite of diversion. And those spreads will buy their supplies here. It'll be more convenient than Buckley, over to the southwest, which is hard to come by from the Coronado and its branches. They do their buying at Buckley now, but soon they'll do their buying here."

"Son, you done got me plumb hornswoggled!" gulped Webb.

Lane grinned. "Andy, it's sort of got me hornswoggled, too," he admitted. "The possibilities are a bit staggering. Remember what they told us in Buckley: that the railroad is building west less than two hundred miles to the east of here. They figure to cut through north of these hills, but I'll bet a hatful of pesos that if a first-rate, growing town springs up here they'll swing south and come through this way. I dreamed of owning a cattle spread some day, but all of a sudden I got bigger notions. You and I are going to own a town! Yes, we're going to build a town on this mesa, and we're going to own the land it's built on. We'll lease or rent, never sell, and we'll be sitting pretty for life, aside from the good we'll be doing a lot of folks."

Old Andy slapped his thigh with a horny hand. "By gosh, it's a plumb prime notion!" he exploded. "Sure we'll build a town, and we'll build a big school, too. I never had a chance to get much education — sometimes I hardly know what you're talking about when you use big words — and I've missed it lots of times. We'll fix it so the kids hereabouts will get their share of book learning. Uh-huh, we'll build a school."

"We sure will," Lane applauded. "And a hospital, and we might even build a church, the kind of church where all sorts of folks can go and talk things over and figure out ways to do good for each other and other folks. I never paid much mind to churches, but that sort of a church appeals to me."

"Hits it off with me, too," said Webb. "A sort of meeting-house church where everybody is welcome. It's a prime notion. That sort of a church will go fine with the school."

Until far into the night the partners talked and planned. Suddenly an idea hit old Andy.

"Mort," he said, "what in blazes are we going to name that town?"

"Andy, you've already named it," Lane chuckled in reply. "You've been talking 'graves' ever since we landed here. We're going to name our town Grave Town!"

CHAPTER IV

Webb and Lane had plenty to do the next day. They took measurements, ran lines and built monuments. After discussing the matter, they descended to the level ground below the mesa and ran more lines.

"The mesa won't be big enough to hold everything," Lane explained. "Folks won't want to live over close to where the hills begin. It will be hotter'n blazes there, with the sun beating back from the cliffs. And we don't want the houses all cluttered together; give 'em room to spread out. Every house should have ground for a garden patch and to raise chickens and hogs. And space for a barn and other outhouses."

"Feller, she's going to be a town!" old Andy chuckled.

"You're darn right she is," Lane said. He straightened his back to gaze eastward.

"And there's something else I'm considering," he added. "As I said, I'm willing to bet the railroad will come here. And it's quite likely that they'll make this a division point with a yard and a roundhouse and shops."

"And loading pens," Webb observed.

"That's right," Lane agreed. "The herds coming up the Coronado will load here and cut a lot of miles off their drive. And that will mean eating houses and so forth close to the sidings. We'll need plenty of land. This down here is good range, and somebody might take a notion to get title to it. Then we'd be hemmed in, and we don't want that. No sense in us missing any bets."

It was nearly sundown before the task was complete, and both were dog tired. But again they sat and talked until far into the night.

As a result of their prolonged gabfest, the prospectors were awake a little later than usual: but the sun hadn't been up long when they got under way.

"We won't take the roundabout route we did coming up here," Lane decided. "Didn't matter then — we had all the time there was — now we've got things to do. We'll cut straight across the rangeland, south by a bit west, till we hit the Buckley trail."

That decision was to have violent and long-lasting repercussions.

The going was easy and they made good time. About mid-morning Lane estimated that they were only a few miles from the trail that ran south to Buckley.

"Well, looks like we're going to have company," Webb suddenly remarked.

Following the direction of his gaze, Lane saw three horsemen riding up from the south-east, and riding fast.

" 'Pear to be heading straight for us," Webb observed a little later. "Maybe want to have a gabfest."

As the horsemen drew near, Lane and Webb slowed their pace and then drew rein.

The three riders came on. The foremost was a big beefy middle-aged man with a square, blocky face, a bristling moustache and a truculent and suspicious eye. He pulled up a half-dozen paces distant; his companions, lean, efficient-looking men in cow country garb, jostled to a halt beside him.

"What are you tramps doing on my range?" he demanded arrogantly in a rumbling voice.

Despite his usually sunny disposition, Mort Lane had a rather quick temper; the man's tone ruffled it. However, his voice was quiet as he replied:

"We're just passing through. And you say

this is your range? I looked over a land map down in Buckley a while back, and it 'peared to me all this section up here is open range — state land."

"State land, nothing!" the other exploded. "I've run cows on this range for forty years, and my dad did before me."

"That so?" Lane countered. "Well, take a mite of advice; get title to it before somebody lifts a chunk from under your nose."

The remark seemed to infuriate the other man. "Don't give me none of your lip, you range tramp!" he bawled. "Get the blazes back where you come from before I use this quirt on you!"

"Hope that quirt's got a smooth handle," Lane remarked mildly.

The other gaped. "What the devil you talking about?" he demanded.

"Well, if it's smooth, if won't hurt so bad when I ram it down your throat!" Lane explained.

With a wordless bellow, the man grabbed for the big gun swinging low on his right thigh. Then he "froze" grotesquely. His two companions also went rigid. They were staring into two black muzzles that yawned hungrily toward them.

Mort Lane spoke, all the softness gone from his voice. "Mister," he said, "I don't know who you are or what you are, but I'm giving you some more advice — turn those bronks and trail your twine away from here — *fast!*" The other hesitated, his mouth contorted with rage, but the ominous double click of the cocking hammers decided him. He whirled his horse.

"This ain't finished," he said over his shoulder, his voice thick with anger. "I'll be *seeing* you again!"

"Take a good look," Lane advised. "Get going!"

"And don't forget, this saddle gun packs a hefty wallop and carries a long ways," old Andy called significantly as he swung his Winchester to the front. The other did not deign to reply, and kept on riding.

As the three riders grew small in the distance, Webb remarked contemplatively:

"Well, we've made a nice start with our neighbours. Think he'll round up his bunch and come back and exterminate us?"

"Not likely," Lane replied. "Would be too much like cold-blooded murder, and I don't figure that crusty gent would go in for anything like that. But I've a feeling we haven't seen the last of him," he added thoughtfully. "Wouldn't be surprised if he's a pretty influential gent in this section, or sets up to be. Old-time baron of the open range. Used to running things his way and doesn't take kindly to being crossed. Expects folks to jump when he cracks the whip."

"Wonder why he braced us that way?" said Webb. "Didn't seem to make sense. You'd think we were pulling up the grass and packing it off."

"Wouldn't be surprised if he's been losing cows and sort of looks sideways at strangers," Lane hazarded. "Pretty close to the New Mexico line here, and there's a market for stolen cattle in the hills over there. Crooked dealers buy 'em from the wideloopers and resell 'em to the reservations or run 'em south to Mexico. Something sure had him on the prod. Well, we might as well get going. Ought to hit the trail in another hour."

Lane was not far off in his estimate. The rest of the trip to Buckley was uneventful, and they reached the town shortly after sundown.

As Lane predicted, they had no trouble securing title to the mesa and a two-mile-wide strip flanking it on the east, south and west, although it took a little time.

"Looks like your acquisition is pretty close to John Bruton's holdings, or what he claims as his holdings," the recording clerk who filled out the necessary papers observed, glancing at a land map that hung on the wall.

"Who's John Bruton?" Lane asked.

"The biggest cattleman in the section," the clerk replied. "He's an old-timer and has just about run things hereabouts for quite a few years. An uppity old bird but a top cattleman. Owns a lot of land. Claims a lot more, almost up to the Espantosa Hills. Reckon he doesn't claim them. Can't understand why anybody would want to," he added, with a curious glance at the two owners of the apparently unprofitable area.

"What sort of a looking jigger is Bruton?" Lane asked.

"Big fellow," replied the clerk. "Got a red face, sort of square-shaped, and blue eyes. Wears a moustache. Hair kind of greying. He owns the Lazy B."

Lane nodded thoughtfully. Outside the office, he observed to Webb:

"So the jigger we had the run-in with up there *is* the big skookum he-wolf of the section. Had a notion maybe he was. Oh, well, it doesn't matter to us; we're not in the cattle business."

Having made sure of their title to the desired land, they filed their claims and had their specimens assayed. There was a little trouble filing for Pedro Lopez, but after discussing the matter the recorder agreed to allow the filing, after Lane explained:

"We'll have the court appoint a trustee to look after his interests till we locate him and get him here."

The assay showed the ore to be of astonishing richness. The assayer grew quite excited. Lane grinned at him teasingly, then divulged the whereabouts of the strike.

"You can pass the word around whenever you've a mind to," he said.

"I will, but not before I get together an outfit and head for the hills," the assayer promised.

Next they visited the local bank, secured an interview with the president and showed him the assayer's report.

The banker also grew excited. "We'll send a mining engineer up there to look over the ground right away," he said. "If things turn out as they appear to be — well —"

They left the bank with a promise of practically unlimited credit, if the engineer's report was favourable.

"It's a regular Mother Lode!" chortled Andy Webb. "Pardner, things are going to boom!"

They did. The news of the strike spread like wildfire. Prospectors swarmed into the hills. Claim after claim was staked. The main lodes extended for miles, and there were offshoots almost as rich. And after the vanguard of the miners came the business people who saw opportunity in their various fields.

Mort Lane staked off about a third of the mesa next to the hill slopes.

"Outside this line and down on the rangeland for a mile in any direction the land's for shacks and cabins and houses for folks to live in," he announced. "Outside this line the land is free. First come, first served. Inside is the business section of Grave Town. Folks wanting to set up business establishments are expected to pay for the privilege."

The business people paid, paid gladly and well. Lane leased the first plot with the stipulation that a building be started within an hour. It was started within half an hour — a saloon.

Lane and Webb hired a crew of competent hard-rock men to develop their claims, old Andy supervising the work. Lane looked after their interests in town.

Grave Town grew like a stack of chips behind four aces. Streets were laid out. Graders and scrapers slashed and tore through the thickets. The air hummed to the rasping of saws, the ringing of axes and the click of hammers. Wagons loaded with lumber and supplies rumbled up the slopes to the mesa. Road builders were busy constructing a wide thoroughfare into the hills and up the canyon to the mines. The first bar in the first saloon, canvas-roofed till the shingles could be nailed in place, was a wide board laid across two barrels. The first dance hall had no roof at all for a while, but nobody seemed to miss it. The mesa beyond the growing business section was dotted with tents, lean-tos, and hastily thrown together shacks. These were swiftly replaced by more substantial dwellings as supplies and materials rolled in. Before a month had passed there were false fronts on Main Street, and windows of plate glass.

"We've taken in enough on leases and advance rents already to get our claims producing properly without borrowing a cent," Lane told his partner. "Now we'll take advantage of the credit the Buckley bank offered. And this will be your chore, seeing as you know all about it. Arrange for setting up two big stamp mills to crush the ore and extract the metal. I want six-stamp batteries in them. We'll crush our own ore and we'll crush for the other claims. When the development warrants it, we'll build more. Get busy, partner!"

Andy Webb got busy. He contracted for

the necessary machinery and equipment and paid a bonus for quick delivery. A swarm of masons and carpenters began erecting the gaunt, towering buildings that would house the batteries. Within little more than another month, the grinding rumble and roar of the stamps doing their ponderous dance in the battery boxes quivered in the air.

CHAPTER V

About this time, Mort Lane received a surprising letter from the McMullen County authorities, to whom he had written relative to the missing "Pedro Lopez."

Judging from the data and description you provided us (wrote the McMullen people) we would say that the individual in question is one Miguel de Alba who was returned here for investigation by the Texas Rangers. Two days after he was brought here, de Alba broke jail and escaped. He might as well have saved himself the trouble, for the grand jury, after weighing the evidence, refused to indict, holding that de Alba undoubtedly shot in self-defence, to rid the community of an undesirable character. Nobody knows where he went. Presumably to Mexico, although we understand he is a Texas citizen. He can stay there so far as we are concerned. We have no further interest in him.

"Oh, well," said Webb, "chances are he'll show up sooner or later, maybe here — everybody all over the country 'pears headed this way. If he don't, we'll try and track him down in *mañana* land."

Lane agreed, and de Alba was dismissed for the time being; the partners had other things to think about, and plenty of business in urgent need of attention.

Among other things, Grave Town was feeling its oats. Newcomers were arriving from all over Texas, and from other states as well. Arizona, Kansas, Oklahoma, and even California each sent its quota of one sort or another, some desirable, some not. Mexico, and sections farther east, were not left out of the picture. Grave Town's population was becoming a heterogeneous one, to put it mildly.

And as the days, weeks and months sped by, there was no let-up in the boom. The production of the mines steadily increased and new discoveries were constantly made. From end to end of the canyon, the black mouths of tunnels yawned in the northern cliffs. As Andy Webb predicted, there were no gold-bearing ledges to the south. All the veins were to the north. His judgment as to best spots to locate their claims was also justified. The three locations of the Alhambra Mine, as they called their holdings, were the richest in the canyon, although there were others not far behind. And Mort Lane was also right in his contention that the richest "claim" of all was the mesa on which Grave Town stood. And it was growing richer all the time.

Already the "residential" section was spilling over the edge of the mesa and down onto the rangeland at its foot. In deference to repeated urging, Lane reluctantly consented to the erection of saloons and dance halls in the "lower" town, as it came to be called, not without certain misgivings.

"Got a feeling I shouldn't have done it," he told Webb. "Things are sort of getting out of hand as it is, and down there is liable to be a trouble spot sooner or later."

Andy was philosophical about the matter. "Oh, let 'er rip!" he advised. "Progress always goes hand in hand with whiskey, cards and women. She'll cool down after a while."

"Uh-huh, but she's liable to get too hot to handle before she starts to cool," Lane predicted. . . .

One day not long after the conversation between the partners, Grave Town had a distinguished visitor. Old John Bruton, owner of the big Lazy B Ranch, rode up to look the town over with a disapproving eye; and he brought others with him.

Grave Town's first saloon, the one with the board-and-barrels bar, had the not inappropriate name of "The Mother Lode." It was owned by a beefy and enterprising individual, one Bert Haskins.

Haskins had a walrus moustache, a spit curl, and a head for business. Haskins also looked to the future. He quickly decided that the muddle of tents and shacks that was Grave Town would not retain that particular status quo. He proceeded to anticipate the Grave Town that was to be.

He erected a spacious, solidly constructed building to house his establishment and furnished it accordingly. His great mirror-blazing back bar was pyramided with bottles of every shape and colour, and the bar itself was of mahogany. In addition to the inevitable roulette wheels, faro bank, dice and poker tables, he had a long lunch counter and a comfortable dining-room in which excellent meals were served.

In even the roughest frontier community there is always a "better" element, one with more money to spend. Haskins made it his business to cater to that element. He had two tough floor men to keep order, and his bartenders were hired for hardness as well as efficiency in mixing drinks. Haskins saw to it that his games were strictly on the level. He was satisfied with the cut the house took on every hand played and every whirl of the wheels, knowing well that he would come out ahead in the long run by operating straight games. And he insisted on courtesy and consideration for all patrons of his establishment. Haskins was a genial host and a smart businessman.

Mort Lane dropped into The Mother Lode for a drink and saw John Bruton sitting at a table. He stopped and stared, although not at Bruton. Sitting beside the ranch owner was a hard-faced, lanky individual who had an efficient look about him. He was Sam Harness, Bruton's range boss.

Not that Lane really "saw" Harness, although his glance passed over his face.

Sitting across from Bruton was a girl with hair the colour of ripe cornsilk. She had a full-lipped red mouth, exquisitely moulded, and a flawless complexion. In the wide eyes, very dark in startling contrast to her hair and complexion, was a hint of the arrogance that marked old John's. All in all, the delicate contours of her extremely pretty face were radically different, there was no mistaking the father-daughter relationship.

Mort Lane's first reaction was one of astonishment. How in blazes, he wondered, could a homely old shorthorn like Bruton have a daughter who looked so much like him and still looked the way *she* did! It just didn't seem to make sense.

His next reaction was a mite different. He forgot all about Bruton. She was certainly easy to look at. Her figure, he noticed, bore no resemblance to Bruton's bulky square-shouldered massiveness. She was slender, tall, and wonderfully formed.

The girl looked up, and Lane guiltily realised that he was staring rudely. He flushed as her eyes met his in a glance of cool appraisal. He turned hurriedly and made his way to the end of the bar.

Lane drank something he didn't taste, and ordered another. He toyed with the second glass, debating whether or not to risk a quick look over his shoulder. He didn't see Bruton and Harness get up and leave the table for a moment.

As Bruton and Harness walked toward the back of the room, the girl beckoned a waiter who hovered nearby.

"Who is the tall black-haired man standing at the end of the bar?" she asked casually.

"Why, miss, that's Mr. Mort Lane," the waiter replied. "He's one of the partners who made the gold strike here. He owns a half-interest in the Alhambra Mine, the richest of them all, and he just about owns this town."

"Thank you," she said, and regarded Mort Lane's back with quickened interest.

Lane couldn't take it any longer. He chanced a quick glance over his shoulder. His eyes met the girl's squarely. A shadow of a smile moved her red lips before she dropped her lashes. Mort Lane breathed deeply, and turned back to the bar as he saw Bruton and Harness crossing the room toward the table.

A few minutes later the trio left the saloon. At the door the girl looked back. Again their eyes met, and again a fleeting smile shadowed her lips.

Bert Haskins, the owner, strolled over to where Lane stood.

"Know the big feller who just went out the door?" he asked.

"Name's Bruton, isn't it?" Lane replied.

"That's right," said Haskins. "He owns the biggest cattle ranch in this section, has sort of run the section for a good many years. Figure he doesn't take overly kindly to what's going on up here."

"Why not?" Lane asked, although he knew very well why not.

"Oh, Bruton holds his comb pretty high and is set in his ways," Haskins rejoined. "He's one of the old-time barons of the open range and doesn't like change. He says things like this gold strike ruin the country. Bring all sorts of bad characters into a section and cause trouble. His kind would keep the whole country to themselves and to blazes with everybody else. Reckon he's on the prod 'cause he sees some of it slipping away from him. That was his range boss with him, Sam Harness, and his daughter Helen. Girl's sort of pretty, don't you think? Prettier than her dad, anyhow; he's a ringy old shorthorn for fair. He had a good-looking wife."

Lane had to chuckle at the way Haskins talked. "He hasn't any wife now?" he asked.

"Bruton's a widower," Haskins answered. "Wife died quite a few years back, when the girl was just a little tad. Bruton never remarried. Helen's an only child. Quite a few young cowhands, and others, that would like to marry her, but I reckon she's after bigger game. The Brutons never were much for playing for small stakes."

"You 'pear to know considerable about them," Lane remarked.

"Oh, I was born and brought up in this section," Haskins explained. "Known the Brutons ever since I can remember. Seen old John lots of times, but never did much talking with him."

With a nod he strolled away again. Lane finished his drink and left the saloon. He had work to do.

CHAPTER VI

John Bruton rode back to his big white ranch-house in a bad temper, and thoughtful. His daughter, familiar with his moods, left him severely alone. Sam Harness also was silent, and bided his time. He wasn't afraid of old John and knew how to handle him. Helen wasn't afraid of anything.

John Bruton was a proud man. Proud of his family background, proud of his possessions, proud of his own proven ability. For many years he had ruled his part of the country with an iron hand. He elected county officials, said who should represent the section in the Legislature and the halls of Congress. His neighbours deferred to him, valued his opinions, looked to him for advice. He was respected, liked by some, hated by others, and feared a little by nearly all. He could be kindly and generous, but he wouldn't stand for being thwarted, and when he struck he struck hard. In short, for many years he had been a law unto himself, and he sincerely believed in his own infallibility.

Bruton was supremely satisfied with conditions as they were and considered them best for all concerned. Progress he looked upon as plain foolishness; the things Grave Town typified were anathema to John Bruton.

However, Bruton was no fool; if he hurt his head butting it against a stone wall, he didn't keep on butting. He proceeded to do something about the wall. Grave Town had given him more of a jolt than he liked to admit. No matter how he might feel about it, Grave Town was there. He couldn't move Grave Town, but he could do something to prevent further encroachments on his domain. After getting back to the ranch-house, he held a conference with Harness, who had been his associate and confidant for many years. Harness, though himself a settled old-timer, was a bit more far-seeing than his boss; Harness was willing to admit that a possibility might very well become a fact, unless its development was curbed in time.

"John," said Harness, "that fellow Lane — oh, it was Lane, all right; couldn't have been anyone else from your description of him — gave you some sound advice out there on the range, when he told you you'd better get title to what you claim as your holdings. I've told you the same thing before now, but you wouldn't listen. If you'd done as I advised, this thing wouldn't have happened. Then the Espantosa Hills would have been private property and you'd have owned the metal rights, under Texas law, and nobody would have been nosing around there. Lane told you straight."

"I'm afraid maybe you're right, Sam," Bruton admitted heavily. "I figured the young whippersnapper was just being smart-alecky."

"He wasn't," said Harness; "and if you hadn't got your bristles up you'd have realised that he *was* right."

"I wish I'd taken the chance and throwed down on him!" growled Bruton.

"Well, from what the boys who were with you told me about how those guns just sort of 'growed' in his hands, I figure you were smart not to try it," Harness replied drily. "You're pretty good, but you're no quick-draw man, as you might as well admit. Lane would have killed you, and he'd have come out on top at the showdown. You braced him on state land. There's a limit to what even you can get away with, John."

Bruton growled and sputtered, but he

didn't argue the point.

"All right," he said, "I'll get busy and get title. I'll write to Leverett over to the capital; he'll shove the matter through the Land Office in a jiffy; there won't be any trouble."

It was a wise decision; there was just one thing wrong with it: Bruton waited a mite too long.

While her father was bothering about land matters, Helen Bruton was pondering other things. She had been impressed by Mort Lane's rugged good looks when he walked into The Mother Lode, and she did not fail to notice his obvious interest in her. When she learned who he was, her own interest increased. In Mort Lane she suddenly saw opportunity.

Although born and brought up in cattleland, Helen had never particularly cared for it. Her school years in a great eastern city had increased her aversion to the rough west Texas country. She had gotten a taste of "civilisation" and liked it.

She knew well, however, that John Bruton was wedded to the land of his birth and could never be persuaded to leave it. And the prosperity of all her acquaintances was dependent on the cow business or its adjuncts. If she married one of them, she could never hope to get away from her distasteful surroundings.

Mort Lane, she felt, was different. He was on the way to becoming a very rich man and he wouldn't be tied to Grave Town, or to Texas, for that matter.

She knew her father had no use for Lane, but that troubled her little. What John Bruton liked or disliked was a matter of total indifference to his daughter. Her own interests came first, although she was always careful not to let him know it. Her task, as she saw it, was to get Mort Lane definitely enthralled. She had enough faith in her undeniable personal charm to believe she could.

CHAPTER VII

Grave Town was no exception to the general run of boom mining communities. Its development followed the conventional pattern. First came the miners, then the legitimate business people who catered to their wants. Workers of various types swarmed in — carpenters, masons, clerks, bartenders, musicians, dance floor girls, dealers, hard-rock men, experts in the various fields of mining including mill workers, teamsters and others. Finally came the inevitable "camp followers" who always show up after a strike. The gamblers, the saloon hangers-on, the gentlemen of doubtful antecedents and unpredictable futures who preferred to do their riding between the hours of sunset and sunrise, and the women with too bright eyes and too red lips. Grave Town got them all, and accommodated them. The acrid tang of powder smoke began to mingle with the smell of tobacco smoke and spilt whiskey. Grave Town's busy hum heightened to a sinister roar.

Lane had been right when he had predicted that the trail herds coming up the Coronado Trail would lay over at Grave Town. And when a big one rolled in, Grave Town howled. The cowhands were a wild and hardy lot, and after days of dust and heat and contrary cow critters, they welcomed a night of diversion and proceeded to make the most of it.

There was one man to whom Lane had leased a plot of land in the lower town below the mesa with certain misgivings. His name was Jess Rader and he wanted to open a saloon. He was a gaunt, uncommunicative individual with black eyes and a lean, tight-lipped face that never seemed to move a muscle. However, he was courteous and well spoken, apparently a man of some education.

Rader wanted to buy his land outright and argued the point; but Lane was adamant in his refusal and Rader finally, albeit reluctantly, signed a lease. Lane felt that Rader didn't take kindly to being thwarted and wouldn't forget. He also experienced a premonition that he should have turned Rader down cold.

Rader's establishment was not so well furnished as Bert Haskins' Mother Lode, but it was almost as large. His employees, from bartenders to swampers, appeared to be cold propositions. And Rader's First Chance rapidly became the hangout of the least desirable element of Grave Town.

Also, for some unknown reason, the visiting cowhands took to Rader's place. And it was the visiting cowhands' liking for the First Chance that was responsible for Grave Town's first serious ruckus.

A big herd of cattle wearing the Circle T brand rolled up from the lower Big Bend country. The Circle T cowboys were a rough lot from a rough country. Their trail boss was a big, keen-eyed man named Bill Fuller, who had been around considerable.

Fuller and several of his hands got into a poker game with a couple of strangers. The rest of the Circle T bunch were scattered around the room amusing themselves in various ways.

The dealer, recently hired by Rader, was a cold-looking individual who handled the cards with unusual deftness. So deft was he that Fuller, though not in a manner to invite attention, got to watching him closely. Perhaps it was the fact that the two strangers were heavy winners that influenced Fuller. Anyhow, as the game proceeded, he gave the dealer considerable attention.

Suddenly Fuller's hand shot out, gripped the dealer's wrist and wrenched his left hand over, palm up.

The dealer wore a ring, an innocent looking ring, on his third finger, but affixed to the band where it circled the inner side of the finger was a tiny mirror, in which the dealer could catch a quick glimpse of the cards as he dealt them.

"Thought so!" bellowed Fuller. "You ornery colddeckin' tinhorn!"

The dealer's right hand streaked across his breast to his left armpit. Fuller's shoulder hunched a trifle.

The two guns blazed almost as one. A red streak leaped across Fuller's cheek. The dealer reeled back in his chair, blood spurting from his shoulder. He slumped sideways to the floor. One of the strangers in the game went for his gun. A Circle T hand bent the barrel of a Colt over his head and put him on the floor beside the moaning dealer.

A burly floor man came bounding across the room, both fists swinging. Fuller weaved aside and with his left hand knocked the floor man head first into a spittoon. Rader rushed in, brandishing a heavy club. Fuller dodged the club and again that lethal left shot out. Rader went down, and stayed there.

A bartender started shooting from the far side of the room. A nearby Circle T hand took care of him with a chair. Three more floor men dived into the row, and ended up on the floor. Things were getting sort of lively. A hurled bottle knocked the faro dealer unconscious. A second bartender came up with a sawed-off shotgun and went down again, minus the shotgun.

And then the Circle T hands, herded together, proceeded to take the First Chance apart. They smashed tables and chairs, shot the big back bar mirror to splinters, shot the bottles off the back bar, shot out the windows, and shot out the lights. In a hurtling wedge, Fuller at the point, they went through the hitting, shooting, squalling crowd and out the swinging doors, taking them off their hinges. Guns were cracking in every direction as they forked their horses. They returned the shots, with interest, whirled their cayuses and skalleyhooted out of town, shooting over their shoulders, bullets buzzing around them like a hive of aroused bees.

A mile outside town they halted to treat minor wounds. Then they rode on, whooping to the stars.

Miraculously, nobody was killed. There were a few punctured hides, more than a few cut heads, black eyes and busted noses; the dealer's shoulder wound was painful, but not serious.

Mort Lane rode down the following morning to look over the damage. He found Rader, with a swollen jaw, making repairs.

"Rader," he told the saloonkeeper, "I don't like the sort of thing that happened here last night."

"Do you think I could have stopped it?" Rader asked.

"No, I guess you couldn't, not after it started," Lane admitted; "but I got it from reliable sources that the row started because one of your dealers was a bit too handy with the pasteboards."

"I fired him," Rader said shortly. "Look here, Lane, this sort of thing is bound to happen now and then. I can't be everywhere and watch everything at once. I don't allow such things in my establishment, but I can't always know all about a man I hire. No matter how hard you try to keep things straight, now and then a crooked dealer or a thieving bartender will slip in and try to feather his own nest. You've been around enough to know such things will happen."

Lane nodded. He couldn't very well contradict Rader's explanation; such things *did* happen.

"All right," he said. "Try and not have it happen again. We'll have the sheriff up here raising ned, and I don't want trouble with the authorities."

There was an ugly glitter in Rader's black eyes as they followed Lane out of the saloon. Jess Rader had ideas and ambitions of his own. Mort Lane didn't know it, but Rader already owned two saloons in the lower town, having recently bought out a man with the provision that the former owner stay on for a while as head bartender and run the place. He was dickering for still another.

Lane rode back to the mesa in a thoughtful mood. Grave Town was certainly getting out of hand; something had to be done about it. He resolved to discuss the matter with Webb.

Old Andy was inclined to discount Lane's estimate of conditions.

"Such things just happen," he maintained. "The boys are only blowing off steam. It ain't serious."

"But if the wrong element gains control here it will be serious," Lane pointed out. "You've heard or read of the Hounds at San Francisco, the Brocius outfit over at Tombstone, the Dutch Henry bunch at Dodge City. What happened there could happen here. We don't want such a bunch to take over the running of things. I've a feeling that Jess Rader is the kind to organise such an element. Before we knew it he'd have the upper hand; then dislodging him would be a difficult chore. Better for us to stay on top of the heap."

"I figure the answer is an organised city government with a mayor, a town marshal and so on," suggested Webb.

"That's an idea," Lane agreed soberly.

"Reckon you'd be the logical choice for mayor," Webb said.

Lane shook his head. "Don't want the job," he replied. "I've got enough on my hands as it is. I think a good solid businessman is the right sort of mayor. Say like Bert Haskins, the owner of The Mother Lode. He's got a good head on his shoulders and he's reliable. As soon as we can get around to it, we'll hold a town meeting and I'll propose Haskins for mayor. Then he can pick out a town marshal, and such other officials as he feels he'll need. If we've got an organisation of substantial citizens pulling together, we won't have to worry about things getting out of hand."

"All sounds sensible," agreed Webb. "We'll get busy on it before long. Well, forget it for the time being: I want you to ride up to the Bonanza Mine at the head of the canyon. I promised them I'd bring you today. They're having trouble up there. They've got a good ledge, almost as good as our Alhambra, but it's a bad one to work. Casing rock is crumbly and the mountain keeps settling. They had a bad fall last night; almost the whole lower drift caved in, and the stuff is still sifting down. Lucky if they don't have trouble on their third drift, too."

"They're well timbered, aren't they?" Lane remarked.

"Sure, good sticks, eighteen inches square; but, son, when a mountain starts settling down, even timbers that size aren't anything. Of course, with proper timbering like they've got, you seldom have sudden falls that kill folks; usually it's gradual and there's plenty of warning. That's the way with the cave-in last night. The sticks started groaning and the rock rumbling, so they emptied the fourth drift in a hurry. They'd hardly cleared it before the stuff really came down. Now, as I said, they're worried about the third. Quite a bit of rubbish has come down there, but the sticks were still holding last night though some of them were pretty well smashed. The Bonanza, you'll remember, is a wet mine, too, just about the wettest on the lode, and if the water happens to get dammed up, when it

74

cuts loose there'll be the devil to pay. Pumps were still working when last I saw 'em though, and even the fourth drift was draining all right. Come on; we'll ride up and take a look."

They saddled up and rode to the gorge.

Finally they reached the Bonanza at the head of the canyon. A number of miners were loafing around the mine mouth, smoking and yarning, for most of the crew had been pulled out of the third and fourth drifts till the mountain decided to behave itself and repairs were made.

The Bonanza was a tunnel mine, as were the majority of the claims in the canyon, its first drift boring into the cliffs at ground level. Below were the other galleries, with still more in prospect. For deep in the earth is almost always the richest portion of a gold and silver ledge.

The superintendent, Jim Knolles, greeted them as they dismounted, and invited them into his office.

"Have a drink and smoke while I get you cap lights and overalls," he said. "Suppose you'll want to look over the fourth drift first. It's a mess down there and the stuff keeps coming; but we'll get it cleaned up in a jiffy. I think the settling is nearly over; nothing really bad since last night when the whole farthest third of the fourth gallery fell in."

After the drinks and the smokes, they donned the overalls and jumpers the super supplied, replaced their hats with caps fitted with lights and entered the mine. They walked along the tunnel for a short distance and took their places in a "cage," a closed-in elevator, and were dropped swiftly down a shaft to the bottom of the mine. From gallery to gallery, one above the other, were vertical ladders affixed to the rock wall. And over them towered the vast web of interlocking timbers that held apart the walls of the gutted lode and supported the tremendous weight above.

The timber web was a gigantic lattice. A great beam, eighteen inches square, was laid on the floor. On it stood verticals five feet high, of similar massiveness, to support a second horizontal, and so on up and up into the empty darkness. The squares formed were a good deal like the framework of a window multiplied a thousand times.

Leaving the cage, they made their way along the fourth drift to where the cave-in began. Here was complete chaos. Vast masses of earth and splintered and broken timbers were piled together in tangled confusion. Some of the massive horizontal timbers had been compressed to a thickness of less than seven inches, mute testimony to the tremendous weight and power of the settling earth. Some of the thick verticals had been mashed into the solid wood of the horizontals to a depth of three inches.

"Plenty of weight up there," old Andy, to whom such sights were nothing new, observed cheerfully.

Lane didn't feel so cheerful about it. It was rather an eerie feeling to be buried hundreds of feet below the surface of the earth, with a mountain slowly settling on one's head.

"Not likely to happen," Webb reassured him. "This sort of thing usually goes slow and easy. Of course, sometimes a big section of the roof does let go all of a sudden."

"And then what?" Lane asked.

"Then," Andy replied drily, "it ain't exactly good judgment to be under it."

CHAPTER VIII

Crews of workers, apparently little affected by the "earthquake" taking place above their heads, were busy cleaning up the mess and replacing the broken timbers. At times they sloshed almost knee deep in water, for the side ditches had been blocked in places, allowing pools to form. Under normal conditions, the water that poured into the drifts from subterranean springs followed the ditches to the sump, from which it was drawn by the ceaselessly working pumps on the surface far above.

"Well, boys," said the super, "I reckon you've seen about all there is to see down here. Suppose we go up to Number Three."

Nobody objected. Lane was glad to get out of that ominous gallery with its creaking and groaning timbers and the sinister grinding and cracking of the settling earth. He was new to quartz mining and had not yet come to the point where he could take all its many hazards in stride. He didn't mind taking a chance when necessary, but if his number was up, he preferred that the showdown should come under the sun or the stars and not in the gloomy depths of the earth.

They retraced their steps to the cage and were drawn to the gallery above. With only Knolles, the super, for company, they walked along the hot, close tunnel. Number Three was a "low" gallery, its web of timbering extending upward for but a short distance.

"And now, Andy," said the super, when they were out of earshot of the cage operator and had not yet reached a point where work was in progress, "I'll tell you why I was so anxious for you to come up here."

"Wondered what you had on your mind," observed the shrewd old-timer. "Figured you didn't just want my advice on what to do about a cave-in. Reckon you know about all there is to know about that, Jim."

"Reckon I do," Knolles admitted. "Okay, I'll tell you. A little farther on, the vein Number Three Drift follows splits in two. One branch is the one the main tunnel follows. The other runs for quite a way almost parallel to the main drift, with just a comparatively few feet of casing rock between the two bores. That goes to almost where the head of Number Three is now. Then all of a sudden it veers sharply, veers away from the main tunnel. I've been closely examining the rock that comes from these two drifts and, Andy, it isn't the same. I know it isn't the same! And that second drift is the richest ore we've yet struck."

Old Andy turned to face Knolles, and by the light of the cap lamps, Lane could see that his eyes were excited.

"And just what are you getting at, Jim?" he asked.

Knolles glanced about the dark bore and lowered his voice, although nobody could possibly hear what he had to say.

"Andy," he answered, "I believe it's a blind lead!"

"The devil you say!" exploded Webb.

"That's just what I mean to say."

"But wait a minute, Jim. Mort is sort of new to this quartz mining business. Reckon I'd better wise him up to just what a blind lead is.

"It's like this, Mort," he continued. "A blind lead is a ledge that doesn't crop out on top of the ground — never shows on the surface. There ain't no way to know where to look for such a lead, but sometimes you stumble on one by accident, while sinking a shaft or driving a tunnel. Sometimes you hit on one in a developed mine, and even the owners and the miners don't always get hep to what it is. Maybe this is one of the times, if Jim's hunch turns out a straight one. Well, we'll see."

"I think it is a straight one," said Knolles, "but I want to be sure. That's why I sent for you, Andy. You know more about rock than anybody in this section. If you say I'm right, I'll know I am. And," he added with significance that was lost on Lane but not on Webb, "I know you and Mort are absolutely straight shooters; I wouldn't have taken a chance on anybody else I know."

"You won't be taking any chance," Webb returned. "Is this where she branches?"

"That's right," said Knolles. "We turn left here. Notice how this bore parallels the original Number Three for a long way; then it veers. Up beyond where she turns the boys are working."

Webb nodded but did not otherwise reply as they turned into the narrower gallery; his attention was fixed on the walls and floor of the tunnel. From time to time he would hold his cap light close to the glistening rock, muttering to himself.

Lane, who was familiar with all his partner's moods, could see that the old man was labouring under a suppressed excitement. Several times he heard him mumble in his whiskers:

"It ain't Bonanza rock! By gosh, it *ain't* Bonanza rock!"

Knolles, walking beside Lane, said nothing. His face was tense, his eyes glowing, and he breathed as one who had run fast and far. Lane didn't know for sure what it was all about, but he felt his own pulses quicken in sympathy. Such held-in excitement was infectious.

Suddenly old Andy halted dead in his tracks, gave his whiskers a vicious yank and swore a complicated, double-barrelled oath.

"Knolles," he said, "it *is* a blind lead! Hanging wall — foot wall — clay casings — everything complete! And this rock is a heck of a sight richer in gold content than the Bonanza rock, and that ain't nothing to sneeze at. Mort, come here! I want you to shake hands with a millionaire!"

Lane took the hand the grinning Knolles extended to him and shook it warmly.

"And now," he suggested, "suppose you fellows tell me just what this is all about. I'm comparatively new to the mining business, you know, and there are angles I'm not altogether familiar with. I'm beginning to get a vague notion about this one, but I want to hear it explained in technical terms."

"It means just this," said Webb: "this lead, or vein of gold-bearing ore, is public property. It holds its way independent of the Bonanza vein, sort of cutting diagonally through it, paralleling their ledge for a while and then, as Knolles says, shooting off in another direction. As I said, it is enclosed in its own well-defined casing rocks and clay. Both ledges, the Bonanza and this one, are perfectly well defined, and it's easy to show which belongs to the Bonanza people and which doesn't. So Knolles, as the discoverer of the lead, has a perfect right to take possession, record it and establish ownership. The Bonanza people will have to stop taking rock from it. What Jim will do is strictly in accordance with mining law and mining custom. Nothing unethical about it. He's the discoverer of a fine gold-bearing ledge, that's all, and it's his by right of discovery. Understand now?"

"Reckon I do," Lane agreed. "I had a notion it was something like that, but I wanted to be sure. Congratulations, Knolles. Couldn't have happened to a finer fellow."

"Much obliged," said Knolles, "and now you fellows listen. I want strong backing in this proposition — that's the chief reason I called you both up here. I was certain about the rock, although I wanted Andy to verify

83

it. I want you two to go into this with me. We'll file and record three claims. That's the way I want it. What do you say?"

"Well," smiled Lane, "much obliged! We're with you till the last cow's branded!"

"My sentiments exactly," chuckled Webb. "Now, Knolles, I want to go up Number Three tunnel to its head. Want to make sure there ain't any more of these maverick ledges around."

"Okay," nodded Knolles as they turned and retraced their steps. "It's a bit rough up there; some falls last night, nothing bad. Reckon we can risk it."

Thirty minutes later they entered the main gallery and proceeded for some distance with only the ominous groaning and creaking overhead to break the silence.

"Just a skeleton crew working in here today," Knolles explained the unwonted stillness. "They're taking care of some shoring and deepening the ditches. This is the wettest gallery of them all. Springs seem to come through everywhere, from the west. None come through the east wall."

"To be expected," said Webb. "The east wall, which is the west casing rock of *your* mine, is tough, close-grained stuff. To the west of this bore is the regulation crumbly casing mostly found in the canyon. That was one of the things that made me see first off that you had a blind lead. The only example of that kind of casing I've seen in the course of this strike."

After better than half an hour of trudging through the dark gallery, they reached a point where the web of timbering was replaced by a ceiling of solid rock no great height above their heads.

"The vein dips down here," Knolles explained. "We expect to go deep here, driving down east of the fourth gallery. Look ahead; you can see where some stuff came down last night. Nothing like what happened to Number Four. Most of the trouble 'pears to be west of here. I've a notion Number Three will escape anything bad."

"Hope so, seeing that we're in it," said Lane, glancing up as a muffled boom followed by a shuddery grinding sounded from within the uneasy heart of the mountain.

"There's usually plenty of preliminary warning," Knolles replied.

"But not always," added old Andy. "Well, you have to take a chance now and then in this business."

A little later they heard sounds of activity ahead and, rounding a slight bend in the gallery, saw lights winking. A few minutes more and they joined a group of a dozen or so miners shoring the sides of the gallery and widening and deepening the ditches that carried off the water which in many places oozed through the west wall.

Knolles inspected the work, spoke a few words to the miners and then turned to Webb.

"Well, see anything of interest?" he asked.

"Nothing to cause me to change my opinion," replied Andy. "You've got a blind lead, and that's all there is to it. Reckon we'd better get outside and get busy; we've got notices to write out and file. We — what the devil!"

From down the dark gallery had suddenly sounded a low rumble that increased steadily in volume, interspersed by thuddings and crashings. The lamps flickered, and the very walls seemed to rock and shudder.

Louder and louder grew the titanic uproar; then it ceased as suddenly as it had begun and was followed by an utter silence in which the gurgle of water in the ditches sounded surprisingly loud.

It was Lane who broke the stillness. "What was it?" he asked.

"That," said Webb, a queer strained note in his voice, "was a fall. A fall in Number Three." He glanced up at the low ceiling.

"Darned glad we got that solid rock over us," he added. "Otherwise it might have reached to here."

"You mean this gallery is blocked?" Lane asked.

"Mighty liable to be," said the old miner. "Come on; we might as well go see. Nothing else likely to come down. No room for it to drop into," he added with grisly humour. "Let's go!"

With the miners, muttering and swearing, trailing behind them, they hurried back down the gallery. They had gone but a few hundred feet when their way was blocked by a mass of broken stone and splintered timbers that began where the rock ceiling ended.

"A fall, all right," said Webb, "and from the sound of it, it's a big one. Reckon the drift is blocked for maybe half a mile. Well, there's nothing we can do about it. Just have to wait till they dig us out. We may get a mite hungry, but nothing worse, the chances are. They'll dig us out." It was Lane who discovered the real danger that threatened them. He realized that his feet were suddenly surprisingly cold. He bent over to ascertain the cause, and as he did so, his cap light reflected back glassily. He was standing in a film of water that covered the floor. He stared at it a moment, then straightened up.

"Well, if they figure to dig us out, they'd better do it in a hurry," he said quietly. "Why? Don't you see why? The fall has blocked the ditches and the water is backing up here fast. Won't be long till it's ceiling-high."

CHAPTER IX

For a moment dead silence greeted Lane's words: then a storm of exclamations burst forth. And suddenly a man screamed, a high-pitched, shivery scream that rose to a rasping screech.

"We'll drown! God A'mighty! We'll drown like rats in a tub!" His voice broke in a wailing gibber.

Mort Lane shot out a long arm, gripped the miner by his shirt collar and shook him till his teeth rattled.

"Stop it!" he said. "There's nothing gained by going loco. Get a grip on yourself! We're not done yet." His prompt action halted the panic that threatened to sweep the miners.

It was Lane who plunged them into despair, and it was Lane who revived their hopes.

"Knolles," he said, "I believe you told us that other gallery we were in parallels

Number Three and runs comparatively close, right?"

"That's right," answered the super. "Along here and almost to the head of the gallery; I'd say there isn't much more than twenty feet of casing rock between the two."

"Then," said Lane, "we've got a chance. All we have to do is break through the rock and into the other gallery before the water rises high enough to drown us. It won't be easy, and we may have mighty little time, but it's a chance."

"By God, you're right!" exclaimed Knolles. "Plenty of tools up here, and powder, too. Come on, boys; grab your picks and sledges and drills."

"But as near the head of the tunnel as possible," said Lane. "The floor slopes down this way, and up there's where the water will get deep last. Jim, can you figure about where the other drift begins to veer away from this one?"

"Pretty close," replied Knolles. "I'd say it begins to change direction about fifty feet or so this side the head of Number Three."

"We mustn't go beyond where it begins to veer," Lane pointed out. "There the wall between would rapidly get thicker. You name the spot and we'll get busy."

Knolles led the way back up the tunnel.

He paused to estimate the distance to the head of the drift and walked on a few more steps.

"I don't think we'd better risk going any further," he decided.

"Okay," Lane said. "Bring up the tools and let's get to work; we haven't any time to waste. Be careful to slope the floor of the cut upward; we must have the charges of dynamite above water when we set the final blow."

Lane spoke cheerfully, but he knew, as did the others, that their chance of winning the race against the rising water was slight indeed. They had to cut through twenty feet of living rock with only manual tools; the steam drills that would have greatly facilitated the chore were, of course, useless; the fall had broken the steam feed lines. But anything was better than just sitting around waiting to die.

Under the crashing blows of picks and sledges wielded by brawny arms, the rock began to come down in showers. They drove an opening wide enough for three men to work abreast. Mort Lane led the attack, wielding a heavy sledge, his strokes falling with the precision of a machine. After a while he stepped back to give place to another man while he caught his breath. He glanced down the tunnel, and his cap light winked back at him.

"Here comes the water," he said to Knolles. "It's rising fast."

"Too fast!" muttered the other. "Well, I was a millionaire for a few hours, anyhow."

"Don't worry; you're going to live to spend a million," Lane told him. "We'll whip this thing yet. By the way, we'd better pile up some slabs of rock against the wall and put the dynamite boxes on top. Don't want the stuff to get too wet. Waterlogged dynamite acts funny sometimes. And we're going to need it in good working shape. We'll dig through as far as we can before the water gets too deep; then we'll have to put in a big charge and try and blow what's left. We'll never be able to cut all the way through with the tools."

Knolles ordered a couple of men to fetch the explosive and place it beyond reach of the water. They hurried to obey. A few minutes later one came back, his face mirroring consternation.

"Boss," he said, "there's plenty of powder sticks and plenty of caps, but there ain't a foot of fuse. We used the last we had this morning; the night shift was supposed to bring in some coils with them when they came on."

Knolles stared at him. "My God!" he exclaimed, "what're we going to do?"

Lane thought a moment. "I believe I've got it," he said: "a trick we used to use sometimes when we were blowing out waterholes on the range. I don't recommend it for a regular thing, but in an emergency it'll sometimes work. Only we'll have to risk it with makeshift materials this time," he added grimly. "Lucky I'm wearing my guns and cartridge belts. Come on farther up the bore — we're already in water down here — and hold a light for me."

First he took off his shirt and tore it into slender strips. Then with his teeth he wrenched the bullets from a number of his forty-five cartridges, carefully emptying the powder from the shells. He dampened the strips of shirt and sprinkled the powder liberally over them, working it into the substance of the cloth with his fingers. Knolles watched him with apprehensive interest.

"My God!" he said at length, "do you mean to tell me you're going to try and set off a dozen sticks of dynamite with those things? They're liable to burn in a flash, and anybody who lights them will be blown clean to the outside!"

"Guess I'll have to risk it," Lane replied composedly. "Jim, there isn't much choice.

Might as well get blown up as drown, and if we don't break through, that's what's going to happen to all of us. You know it well as I do. But I think the darn things will behave right. They're not bad for makeshift fuses. Well, that should do it. We'll put 'em with the dynamite till the time comes to use them. Let's get back to the cutting. Here comes the water up here!"

They returned to where the picks and sledges were thudding steadily. The water was already knee-deep in the tunnel. Lane took his place at the head of the cutting again; Knolles watched him admiringly.

"That big jigger doesn't know his own strength," he remarked to Webb. "He brings down more rock in a minute than anyone else does in three. Look at him swing that sledge! But the rock's getting harder — we're almost through the crumbly casing and up against that which walls in the blind lead. Andy, it's going to be close. Between you and me, I doubt if we can make it in time. And everything will depend on the blow breaking through. Hope to God I haven't underestimated the thickness of that wall. If I have, well —"

Webb nodded soberly. "It don't look good," he agreed. "Don't matter so much about an old coot like me, but it's a shame for you young fellers who are just beginning to live."

"Oh, maybe we'll make it," Knolles answered, voicing a confidence he didn't feel. "Anyhow, we'll keep slogging away for so long as we've got any air to breathe."

The rock was getting harder and closer-grained. The picks would no longer make any impression on it. Only the thudding blows of the heavy sledges would crack and loosen the stubborn quartz, and the arms that wielded them were growing weaker. The water sloshing on the floor of the cut also hampered the workers. And in the main gallery it was almost breast deep. Finally Lane called a halt.

"Time for the drills," he said. "No use pounding that stuff any more. Drive the holes and we'll load 'em, as many as we have time for. Go to it, you steel men; the water's getting higher by the minute."

Soon the musical ring of hammers on the drill heads echoed from the walls. The sharp drills bit into the stone, driving the holes deeper and deeper. Lane anxiously watched the slow rise of the water. In the gallery it was now almost shoulder high on himself, and he was considerably above average height. Another hour and two short men were sent to the head of the tunnel. Old

Andy, with water almost to his chin, stubbornly refused to budge.

"I can swim," he said. "I'm staying right here till the charges are loaded."

Hole after hole was drilled, and finally Lane again called a halt.

"If this won't do it, nothing will," he said. "Powder men to the front."

Swiftly the greasy dynamite cylinders were shoved into the holes, earth and bits of rock tamped onto them. Lane himself handled the chore of fastening the detonation caps and rigging his makeshift fuse. Finally all was in readiness. Only Lane, Knolles, two more tall men and old Andy remained in the cutting: the others were sent to the tunnel head, where the water was as yet not more than breast high.

Lane arranged his net of fuse with the utmost care. He dampened some of the strips a little more, sprinkled more powder on others. Finally all was ready. He straightened his aching back and glanced around.

"Okay, up to the head of the gallery with you fellows," he said. "I'm all set to light them. Face the end wall and hang on. There's going to be one whale of a concussion when this stuff lets loose, and if you aren't braced for it, you're liable to get slammed around a bit. I've got a feeling it'll break through all right, and if the other gallery isn't full of water, too, we should be okay."

"Uh-huh, if it isn't," muttered old Andy. "Listen, Mort, let me light the thing. I'm old — my time's almost up in any event. You're young, with your whole life before you. Let me light 'em."

Lane patted him affectionately on the shoulder. "Get going," he said. "When I come up the tunnel I'll be in a heck of a hurry, and I don't want to trip over any old coot. So long, pardner; get going!"

Half wading, half swimming, and swearing brokenly, old Andy followed the others to safety.

Lane waited till he was sure they had reached the gallery head; then he fumbled a match from a tightly corked bottle and struck it. The tiny flame flickered up brightly. He bent over and applied the flame to the fuse, and held his breath as he did so. If he had underestimated the amount of dampening, the fire would race along the cloth and he would be blown to pieces before he could escape the exploding charge.

The fuse sputtered, smouldered, flared up with a quick and terrible burst of flame, then settled to a steady crawling flower of fire. Lane turned and sloshed his way down the cutting. The water in the gallery was over his shoulders, almost to his chin, in fact. He tripped and floundered, his progress frightfully slow. Behind him that crawling flower of fire might be quickening. He surged forward with all his strength.

As he climbed the tunnel the depth of the water lessened and he made better progress; but he was panting for breath and well nigh exhausted when at last he reached the end wall and braced against it alongside Knolles and Webb.

"Thank goodness you made it!" quavered old Andy. "Is it all —"

His voice was drowned by a thunderous roar followed by a thudding and crackling. The tunnel blazed with light. The water rushed to the end wall in a tidal wave, submerging them, and as it surged back they were struck a hammer blow by the displaced air. Webb was swept off his feet, but Lane seized his collar as he went under and dragged him erect.

Dazed, bewildered, half drowned, the miners grovelled against the rock wall, crying and cursing. Then Lane felt a current of cool air fan his face. He let out a jubilant shout.

"We did it!" he cried. "Feel the fresh air

coming in. We blew the wall. Now if the hole is just big enough to let us out! Come on, everybody; the water's getting deeper by the second. Anybody who can't swim? Okay, we'll help you. Let's go!"

Everybody except Lane, Knolles and a couple more six-footers did have to paddle and swim to the cut. Lane assisted one man who couldn't swim, Knolles another. Finally, when it began to look as though they were done for, after all, they reached the cutting and sloshed and floundered up its steep floor.

Most of the cap lights were out, but one or two still burned feebly and showed a jagged hole in the drift wall. Lane floundered through and dropped to the floor of the blind lead tunnel. There was no water, and the steady current of air sweeping up the gallery told him it was not blocked.

"Everybody present?" he asked. "Okay, let's get out of here. I want to see the sun again."

"I, for one, never expected to," declared Knolles. Others croaked hoarse agreement.

"And if it wasn't for Mort, we never would have," the super declared with conviction.

This time the bruised and battered and worn-out miners croaked a feeble cheer.

Somewhat revived by the fresher air, they

started the weary trudge to the outside. When they reached the point where the tunnel joined with the main gallery of Number Three, they heard voices and the thudding of tools, and no great distance up the main drift they could see lights winking.

"Trying to dig us out," said Webb. "Guess we'd better go up and tell them we're all right. Douse your cap lights and be quiet; we'll have some fun."

He slipped up behind a foreman who was directing the rescue operations, tapped him on the shoulder and said in sepulchral tones:

"You boys looking for somebody?"

The foreman whirled around, stared, and let out a yell that nearly brought the roof down.

"Ghosts!" he bawled, and started to run.

Lane grabbed him as he streaked past and held him. "Take it easy!" he laughed. "We're all okay."

"Gosh, you gave me a start!" quavered the foreman, wiping his damp forehead. "How in blazes did you get out?"

The workers gathered round, babbling questions. "We broke through into the branch tunnel," Lane explained briefly. "Tell you all about it later. Right now let's get topside; we're worn out and starved."

Although it was well past midnight, most of Grave Town was at the mine entrance when they emerged. And that night Grave Town celebrated as never before.

CHAPTER X

Lane and his companions didn't take part in the shindig; they went to bed and slept like drugged men.

Hardly had the excitement over the miraculous escape from the caved-in mine subsided when the sensation of the blind lead broke. Grave Town roared again.

"She's beginning to live up to her name," Webb told Lane the following morning. "Two gamblers shot it out in the lower town last night. We're getting a Boothill started."

"Where'd it happen?" Lane asked.

"In Jess Rader's place."

"I've a notion to close that place!" Lane declared angrily.

"You may run into real trouble if you try it," Webb warned. "Better wait till we get organised and have peace officers to handle such chores. No sense taking the law into your own hands; it's dangerous."

"Something's got to be done," Lane

grumbled. "We can't let things go on this way."

"Son, I know just how you feel, but this is a Texas gold strike town," Webb answered. "It ain't going to be quiet and it ain't going to be peaceful."

"I know that," Lane admitted, "but I don't want it turning into a hell town. I want it to be the sort of a town where decent people can come, people like —" He did not finish the sentence, and flushed a little. It had been on the tip of his tongue to say, "people like Helen Bruton."

Webb was too absorbed in his own thoughts to notice his partner's sudden confusion.

"Just had a talk with Jim Knolles," he announced. "The Bonanza Mine people have made us a proposition. They offer the use of their tunnel and shafts for a percentage of the blind lead's output."

"What do you think?" Lane asked.

"I think it's a good notion," replied Webb. "It'll save the time and expense of driving a tunnel and sinking shafts and will get production going at once. If things work out like I fully expect they will, they'll make a good thing of it, but so what! Live and let live, I say."

"Agreed," said Lane. "We'll get in touch

with Judge Arbaugh down at Buckley and have him draw up the papers. By the way, the Judge says so much money is piling up for our *amigo* Pedro Lopez that being trustee for it is a heavy responsibility. I sure wish we could locate that jigger. So far I haven't gotten a thing from Mexico. Every mayor I wrote to says he never heard of anybody answering his description."

"We've got to find him," agreed Webb. "Maybe he never went to Mexico. Maybe he's in Texas."

"Could be," Lane admitted, "but it isn't likely. He must have felt sure the grand jury would indict him when he busted out of the calaboose, and not knowing it didn't, he wouldn't be apt to stay within the jurisdiction of Texas courts. Well, maybe we'll get a line on him sometime. When I wrote to the Mexican *rurales* I promised a reward for information. The mounted police will keep an eye open, and perhaps they'll run across him sooner or later. Let's go see Knolles; I want to talk with him, and then I think I'll take a little ride."

"Once a cowhand, always a cowhand," chuckled Andy. "Reckon you don't feel just right when you ain't forking a horse."

"Sort of that way," Lane admitted with a smile. He did not confide in his partner that he usually rode in the direction of the Buckley trail, near which sat John Bruton's big ranch-house.

Helen Bruton was very anxious to meet Mort Lane; but she was puzzled as to just how to go about it. She thought of riding to Grave Town and casually "running into him," but decided it might look a bit too obvious. When she heard of Lane's habit of riding the north range and the Buckley trail, she saw an opportunity.

So it was not exactly by accident that Lane, riding across the sun-dappled prairie, saw a graceful figure mounted on a powerful blue moros ride from behind a thicket no great distance away. How was he to know that the moros' sudden exhibition of weaving and sunfishing was induced by his ribs being tickled by the spurs on the heels of a pair of dainty riding boots?

Concerned for the girl, who appeared to be having trouble with the big blue horse, he quickened Rojo's pace and quickly closed the distance between them. Abruptly the moros "swallowed his head" and his rider went flying through the air.

The moros stopped his cutting up, stared in astonishment and uttered an inquiring snort. What kind of a game was this? *He* knew he couldn't throw his mistress if he uncorked his whole bag of tricks for a week of Sundays. But Mort Lane couldn't understand horse talk. And he was too absorbed with anxiety as to what might have happened to Helen to realise that she had landed practically on her feet, the force of the fall expertly broken by her hands. He jerked Rojo to a slithering halt, unforked while the sorrel was still in motion and knelt beside her.

"Are you all right?" he asked anxiously.

She looked a bit dazed but gave him a smile.

"Just shook up a little, that's all," she replied with a realistic quiver in her voice. "I don't know what got into Smoke all of a sudden, he doesn't usually act up that way. He caught me off guard."

With the help of Lane's arm about her shoulders, she sat up, and gave him another smile.

"Thank you, Mr. Lane," she said.

Lane looked surprised. "How come you know my name?" he asked.

"Oh, everybody knows you," she replied. "You were pointed out to me when Dad and I visited Grave Town. You're quite a celebrity, you know, and I heard last night that you saved the lives of a dozen men in a caved-in mine. Begins to seem rescuing folks from distress is a habit with you; just like the knights of old!"

"I didn't do much," he deprecated, "and I reckon I was thinking most of saving my own."

Her smile showed disbelief. Lane hastily changed the subject.

"And you're Miss Bruton," he said. "I didn't have to have *you* pointed out to me. You looked rather out of place in our shack town — sort of like a rose on a slag heap."

"That was prettily said," she replied with a little laugh. "And today I must have looked like a sack of potatoes tumbled out of a wagon."

"If I was sure you wouldn't get hurt, I'd ask you to do it over," he declared. "I don't believe you could do anything ungracefully."

"Even to tumbling off a horse?" she asked with another laugh. "I'm beginning to believe, Mr. Lane, that you must have kissed the Blarney Stone."

"I understand my great-grandmother did," he answered, falling in with her humour. "But I've been told the Blarney Stone is set down below the battlements of Blarney Castle, so that you have to be held by your ankles, head down, to kiss it.

Somehow I can't visualise the old lady in that position."

"Perhaps she wasn't an old lady at the time," Helen replied demurely. "Goodness! I must be a sight! My hair flying every which way, and look at the grass stains on the knees of my nice clean Levi's! Do you disapprove of girls wearing overalls?"

"You look wonderful any way," he declared emphatically.

Helen laughed and sprang lightly to her feet.

"I'll have to be going," she said; "it's late. I think Smoke will behave himself now."

Smoke raised his head and gave her a disgusted look.

"Hadn't I better ride with you, just in case he doesn't?" Lane suggested.

She regarded him seriously for a moment. "Well, you can ride with me to the trail, if you care to," she agreed. "I'd ask you home to have dinner with us, only I don't think it would be advisable right now. I'll have to soften Dad up a bit first. I understand that he and you did not exactly agree, when you met out here on the range."

"I don't think it was anything serious," Lane answered.

"Oh, it was nothing to worry about," she assured him. "Dad is crusty, but he cools down after a while. You must have caught him at a bad moment. Anyhow, he's taking the advice I heard you gave him. He's getting title to all the land up here. Once that is off his mind, I've a notion he'll be in a mood to be reasonable. He'll quickly forget about the matter, and I can handle him."

CHAPTER XI

Lane and Webb had built their house, a roomy one-storey cabin, on the south lip of the mesa, from where they had a splendid view of the rangeland and the mountains beyond. Lane thought it one of the most beautiful vistas he had ever encountered, and he liked to sit on the front porch and gaze out over the prairie shimmering gold and green at noonday or amethyst and smoky purple when the shadows were growing long.

One morning he noted activity on the grassland somewhat beyond where their holding ended. Men on horseback were riding back and forth and a number of loaded wagons hove into view. He couldn't quite make out what was going on. Then he bethought him that one of old Andy's prize possessions was a fine field glass. He got the glass and focused it on the scene of activity. After gazing a moment, he let out a low whistle.

"Andy!" he called, "come out here."

"What's up?" asked Webb as he appeared in the doorway, a skillet in one hand and a dish cloth in the other.

"Want you to take a look at something," said Lane. "There's a bunch running fence down there on the range."

Webb took the glass and focused it to his own vision.

"Darned if they ain't!" he agreed after a long look. "Setting posts and stringing bob wire. Bob wire in this section! Gentlemen, hush!"

"Barbed wire's coming to all sections," Lane replied. "Miles and miles of it up in the Panhandle, and over east. Cowmen are beginning to learn that fenced range is easier to work."

"But it doesn't set well with the old-timers," said Webb. "They hate the sight of wire. Bet John Bruton rares and charges when he hears about it."

"I've a notion it won't do him any good," Lane answered. "Why? Because if that jigger down there is building fence, it means he's got title to a section. You can bet on that."

"Heard Bruton was getting title to everything up to our line," observed Webb.

"Yes, I heard it, too," Lane admitted, a pucker showing between his black brows.

"Looks like somebody beat him to it, up here, anyhow."

"Uh-huh, looks that way," Webb agreed, "but just the same, he'll paw sod."

John Bruton did paw sod when he heard about it. He rode up to the fence building with Sam Harness and seven or eight of his hands. His face was red with anger as he viewed the long line of posts and the taut, gleaming strands.

Standing nearby as Bruton rode up was a slender young man with a good-humoured and exceedingly good-looking face dominated by a pair of gay, laughing grey eyes. He waved a greeting.

Bruton ignored the greeting. He jerked his horse to a halt, the others jostling alongside him.

"What's going on here?" he demanded.

"Building fence," the young man replied composedly.

"Well, you can stop it, and pull up those posts and get out of here!" roared Bruton. "I'm getting title to this land and I ain't having any blasted wire on it!"

" 'Fraid you're a mite late," the other replied. "I've already got title to a section up here. Didn't know anybody else was after it." He smiled pleasantly as he made the announcement, which tended to increase Bruton's anger.

"For half a cent I'd pistol-whip you within an inch of your life!" he declared.

"Don't reckon it would be a good notion to try it," the young man said, the laughter suddenly gone from his eyes but his voice still quiet. "Suppose you take a look behind you."

Bruton instinctively glanced over his shoulder, and saw half a dozen men with rifles cradled in their arms.

"And I might remind you that right now you're trespassing on private property," the young man added. "I don't want trouble with anybody, but if you start some, you're paid for."

Bruton was about to voice a hot reply, but Sam Harness put a restraining hand on his arm.

"Boss, he's right," Harness said in low tones. "If he's got title, you wouldn't have a leg to stand on. Take it easy!"

Despite his rage, Bruton knew that Harness was talking sense. He controlled himself with an effort.

"All right," he said, "but we'll see about this! Come on; let's get out of here."

Bruton did try to "see about it," but it didn't do him any good. The young man,

Barry Curtis by name, had bought and paid for a large section south of the Espantosa Hills. Bruton would acquire everything farther south, but the north pastures were beyond his reach.

"It's all that range tramp Lane's fault," Bruton declared. "Everything was okay till he showed up. I wish he'd stayed in that caved-in mine!"

"That's not a nice thing to say," protested Sam Harness. "I don't see why you have to blame Lane for what happened. And there's no sense in getting on the prod against Curtis, either. He had a perfect right to get title, and you know it. You just didn't move fast enough, that's all. I told you a long while back you ought to get title, but you wouldn't listen."

Old John exploded like an erupting volcano, but he knew it was no use getting mad at Harness. Sam didn't scare.

Harness waited patiently till the flames subsided somewhat; then he took a bottle from a drawer and poured a drink.

"You'll go off some day in a spell like that," he predicted. "Here, have a slug of redeye and cool down. The world ain't coming to an end because you didn't get a chunk of range. You've got more land than you know what to do with as it is."

"Barbed wire!" sputtered Bruton, sucking the drops from his moustache. "Barbed wire in the Guadalupe country! What's Texas coming to, anyway?"

Barbed wire was bad enough, but what was to come was infinitely worse, from John Bruton's viewpoint.

Andy Webb took a great interest in the doings down on the rangeland, which included the building of a comfortable ranch-house, and it was Webb who made an appalling discovery as his glass focused on the myriad of woolly backs rolling out of the east.

"Mort, come here!" he yelled. "You know what? That feller down there is running in sheep!"

Mort Lane received the startling news with equanimity. "I see now why he's fencing his range," he observed. "I've no more use than any cowman has for sheep that are allowed to run loose and destroy grassland, but sheep on a fenced range won't do any harm. If he can stand the blatting woollies, let him raise 'em."

"But this is cattle country," Webb pointed out, "and the cattlemen won't like it one bit, even if his range is fenced."

"Maybe not, but there's no use fighting sheep," Lane returned. "They can lose every battle and still win the war."

"Uh-huh, war," said Webb. "And a cattlemen-sheepmen war ain't anything to joke about."

"You're right there," Lane admitted seriously, "but I don't see why there should be trouble so long as he keeps them fenced in."

Webb wasn't so sure. "I've noticed that when sheep start coming into a section, they keep coming," he said. "And the next jigger to run in a flock may not be so particular about the range being ruined by their eating the grass down to the roots and cutting it with their sharp hooves."

"You're right again," Lane agreed more seriously. He had an uneasy premonition that the latest development would not tend to further his own personal ambitions in a certain direction.

His fears were justified when he met Helen Bruton the following afternoon.

"I'm afraid I'll have to postpone the dinner invitation," she told him ruefully. "Dad's fit to be hogtied, and I don't want to do anything right now to make him worse. I don't see the sense of him getting worked up so over a few sheep, especially when they'll be fenced in.

"I wish that man hadn't brought them here, though," she added, a touch of irritation creeping into her voice. "I don't like to

116

have Dad so disturbed, and to have my plans scrambled. But don't worry; I'll take care of him after a while." Her lips tightened against her teeth as she said it; but instantly she was smiling again.

"Now tell me about yourself," she urged. "Any more trouble with your mines? It must have been terrible, being buried in the ground that way and not knowing whether you'd ever get out. And how is your town coming along? I hear you're building a school. I'm going to ride up there soon. I imagine it's lively. Buckley is so drearily sleepy all the time. I didn't notice it so much until I went away to school, but now I get irritated with its stodginess."

"Really, I can't say as I noticed it particularly," he replied. "Guess I was too busy."

"Tell me about yourself and what you're doing," she repeated.

He told her, outlining his plans for the town and the development of the mines, but making little mention of himself. She listened with flattering attention.

"It would appear you are well on the way to becoming a very rich and famous man," she remarked as he paused, smiling at her.

"Maybe," he admitted, "but I really don't hanker for much; I'll be content with a good living, and maybe a little spread to play around on. I was raised to the cattle business, you know; and once a cowhand, always a cowhand, or so the old-timers say."

"And haven't you any ambition to travel, to see things, to live where things are happening?" she asked.

"Well, I've been around a bit," he answered. "Dad was pretty well fixed until the bottom dropped out of the cattle business. I had a couple of years at college, in Chicago, and I've been to New York and San Francisco and a few other places. Didn't care for them much — too darned crowded and noisy."

Miss Bruton's delicate brows drew together a little. She seemed to hesitate before replying, as if carefully choosing her words.

"But don't you sometimes find all this monotonous and tiresome?"

Lane glanced around at the glowing rangeland, the purple mountains shouldering the sky, the shadowy, mysterious canyons and the towering crags and pinnacles piercing the limitless blue.

"I don't see how it would be possible to find it monotonous or tiresome," he replied slowly. "Always there is change and variety. Each day runs the gamut of beauty, and each night is a breath-taking promise of the wonders to come the next day."

Helen looked at him a little strangely. He meant it. All of a sudden she felt that her task was not going to be as simple as she had supposed.

CHAPTER XII

With his acquisition of an interest in the blind lead, Lane's duties became multitudinous. In consequence, he hired an agent to handle his real estate holdings. That evening, after getting back to town, he dropped in on the agent to discuss some matters.

"The Occidental Saloon has a new owner," the agent announced after they had talked awhile.

"You mean Frank Lerner's place on Mesa Street, down in the lower town?"

"That's right," said the agent. "Lerner has a place in Buckley, you know, and he wasn't satisfied up here. He's a family man, and the business was keeping him away from home too much. So when this fellow Mike Day came along looking for a place to locate, he was glad to sell. They came to me to okay the deal, of course. I liked Day's looks and figured it would be all right."

"What kind of a looking jigger is Day?" Lane asked idly.

"Tall, rather slender build, black hair with a lot of grey in it, black whiskers with grey in them, too. He's well spoken and made a good impression on me."

Lane nodded. "Hope he runs a nice place," he said; "we're getting too many of the other kind, I'm afraid. Think I'll drop in and look him over."

"Hope you won't figure I did the wrong thing," said the agent.

"Walt, if I hadn't felt I could depend on your judgment in such matters, I wouldn't have hired you," Lane replied with a smile. "After all, Judge Arbaugh recommended you, and I don't think the judge is given to making mistakes."

"Thank you," said the agent; "you're a good man to work for, Mr. Lane."

A little later in the evening, Lane did drop into the Occidental, a big, brightly lighted and well appointed place. It boasted a mirrored back bar almost the equal of the one in Bert Haskins' Mother Lode, a couple of busy roulette wheels, a faro bank and poker tables. It was a going place, all right, Lane decided as his glance roved over the crowd. His gaze strayed to the dance floor in the back and stayed there.

"Hoppin' horntoads!" he muttered. "Where did *she* come from?"

A girl was dancing on a table at the edge of the floor, and she danced with the grace of a flower swaying in the wind. The table was littered with bottles and glasses, but her tiny feet disturbed not one. She was small and slender, and her curly black hair framed a small oval face that was blossom-white. Her sweetly formed lips were hibiscus-red, and there was a touch of rose on each soft cheek. On the bridge of her shapely little nose were a few freckles. And she had the biggest and bluest eyes Mort Lane had ever seen.

"What a knockout!" he muttered. "You don't often see anything like that on a saloon dance floor."

Near the table, watching her intently, was a man Lane decided must be Mike Day. As the agent said, he was rather tall, lean and slender. He was bearded almost to the eyes, but the grizzled beard and the crisp moustache were carefully trimmed and combed and seemed to add to rather than detract from his astonishing good looks. His black hair was liberally streaked with grey. About forty, perhaps a little more, Lane decided.

Lane agreed with Walt Slaven, the agent; he also liked Mike Day's looks. Then he forgot all about him and his attention centred on the girl, who was going through an intricate step.

She finished her dance and sprang lightly to the floor, her face bright with laughter at the applause that shook the room. There was a proud look in Mike Day's dark eyes as they rested on her.

From a nearby table a big cowhand, more than a little drunk, lurched to his feet. He strode to the girl and flung an arm around her slender waist.

"Come on, honey; let's you and me hoof it," he rumbled.

The girl deftly disengaged herself from his embrace and stepped back.

"Not now," she said, her voice soft and liquid. "Later, perhaps."

"Aw, come on," urged the cowboy, moving toward her again and reaching out a hand.

Mike Day stepped in front of the girl.

"Not now," he said courteously but firmly. "You have been drinking too much. The lady —"

"Who told you to horn in!" the puncher interrupted roughly. "Out of my way!"

His big hand shoved the other back. The elderly Day caught his balance and gathered himself together, his dark eyes glittering.

But before he could move, Mort Lane stepped between them.

"Hold it!" he dropped over his shoulder to Day. "You're out of your class with this jigger; he's twenty years younger and seventy pounds heavier.

"And, Feller, *you're* plumb out of order," he told the cowboy.

The puncher's face flushed darkly red. He took a menacing step forward, his long arms swinging at his sides.

"Who the devil sent for you?" he demanded truculently. "Sift sand away from here before I skin you up till you look like a fresh hide!"

Mort Lane's grey eyes narrowed a little as they rested on the other's angry face. His own temper was rising.

"Nobody's sitting on your shirt-tail, so far as I can see," he remarked composedly but with a significance that was not lost on the cowboy. His face contorted with anger, he gave a wordless bellow and rushed, fists swinging.

Mort Lane hit him, left and right, hard. He staggered back, blood on his face, shook his bristly red head and charged again.

And again Lane hit him, hard, slashing blows that left their mark. He barged into a table and over it went, scattering bottles and glasses on the floor.

But he was big and he was tough. He caught his balance, boomed his wordless war cry again and charged back, head bent low.

Mort Lane, much the faster of the two, weaved aside to avoid his rush, stepped on a broken bottle and staggered, off-balance, and the puncher caught up with him. There was nothing to do but stand and slug it out.

Lane was a big man, six feet in height and weighing close to two hundred pounds, within twenty pounds, perhaps, of the cowboy, and he was lean and hard from years of desert wandering. His driving punches brought grunts from his opponent.

But he was taking plenty himself. A red spot showed on one cheek bone. There was blood on his lips. His head rang as the other connected solidly with his jaw. He ducked his head and grimly bored in.

A wild flurry of blows, panting breath, hissing grunts. Lane's long right arm suddenly was jarred to the shoulder by the force with which his fist landed. The cowboy reeled back, groaned, whirled around and fell on his face, twitching and writhing and gasping for breath. Lane stepped back, panting.

The four cowhands at the table, who had

been whooping encouragement to their companion, surged to their feet with a storm of oaths. One jerked his gun.

Mort Lane saw the flicker of steel and also "reached," an instant too late.

But he didn't need to bother. The little dancer's foot shot out, and the toe of her slipper caught the cowboy squarely on the sensitive point of his elbow. The gun clattered to the floor. Its owner doubled up with a howl of anguish, gripping his pain-wracked arm between his knees.

Somebody laughed. Somebody else took it up. In an instant the whole room was a-bellow with mirth.

The big redhead, who had gotten to his feet rather dazedly, stared in astonishment. He looked at Mort Lane uncertainly. Lane returned the look, also uncertainly. Neither made any move.

"Feller," the redhead said plaintively, "can you tell me what's so funny about a jigger getting knocked from under his hat?"

Chuckling, Lane told him what had happened. The redhead bellowed louder than anybody else. Then his face hardened and he strode to the offending puncher, who was rubbing his still tingling elbow.

"What's the big notion?" he bawled. "Can't me and this gent have a sociable wring without you jugheads shoving in your two pesos worth? And because he knocked me through myself, don't think any of you bowlegs can do it. Set down there and 'tend to your own business 'fore I take you apart!"

He whirled about, faced Mike Day and held out his hand.

"Sorry, Mike," he said. "I didn't mean no harm; just wanted to dance. It won't happen again. Here's my hand on it."

"Think nothing of it," said Day as they shook hands. "I never forget it's the stuff I sell on my side of the bar that causes all the trouble on this side."

The cowboy turned to Lane. "And that's what I call a regular jigger," he said, jerking his thumb toward Day, and then sticking out his hand again. "Shake, Feller! No hard feelings, and I hope you ain't got none. It was quite a wring while it lasted, wasn't it?"

They shook hands, smiling into each other's eyes. The cowboy flung an arm around Lane's shoulders. "Come on, Feller," he urged. "You and me are going to have a drink together. Feel like celebrating. Ain't been hit so hard since I told Dad I was too big for him to lick any longer, and he showed me I wasn't, with a scantling. Come along!"

Lane paused to speak to the little dancer. "Thank you," he said simply.

"Thank *you*," she replied in her soft voice, and with a smile that showed the dazzling white of her perfect teeth. She nodded in a friendly fashion, glided across to where Mike Day stood and slipped her arm affectionately through his. Lane turned to the big cowboy, who led the way to the bar and bellowed for whiskey.

He chortled in his throat, grinned at Lane, and waved his fellow punchers to come and join them.

The redhead performed the introductions. "The fat one hiding behind the grin is Slim Tompkins," he said. "The one with the sore arm, dadblame him, is Pete Withrow. The beanpole is Silent Simpkins; he never shuts up. The hungry-looking one is Dishwater Bailey. Got up one night half asleep and took a big swig out of what he thought was the water bucket. It was the one the cook emptied his dishwater in. He ain't never been the same since. Me. I'm Val Jackson. I own the Cross C, over to the west of John Bruton's holdings, and these misfits ride for me. I didn't get *your* handle, Feller."

Lane supplied his name. Jackson let out a whoop. "Why, you're the jigger who started these diggin's and who owns the whole shebang!" he exclaimed. "Plumb glad to know you, Lane; I've took a shine to you. Nothing

128

like having a wring with a feller to make you like him, especially if he comes out on top."

"If those are the necessary qualifications, I've a notion you've never had to like many," Lane smiled.

Jackson bellowed with laughter and ordered more whiskey.

Lane finished his drink and said goodnight. "Got a busy day ahead of me," he explained.

"Figure you must have, with all you got to ride herd on," agreed Jackson. "Sure hope we'll see you again. We drop in town ever so often, and I reckon we'll sort of make this place our stamping ground. I like it here."

At the door, Lane paused and glanced back. The little dancer was still standing beside Mike Day. He waved to her and she waved back, and he was struck with the utter grace of every movement she made.

"Yes, she's sure a knockout," he repeated his first impression. "Day's lucky. Reckon he's about twice her age, but he's a fine-looking jigger and appears to be a good deal of a gentleman. Well, I've a notion she saved me from getting an air-hole in my hide. I saw that cowhand pull just a mite too late. He'd have gotten in the first shot, all right, and the first shot very often is the last one. Guess I'm sort of beholden to her."

CHAPTER XIII

The row in the Occidental convinced Lane more than ever that it was high time Grave Town had an organised city government and officials with the authority to deal with disturbances. The result was Grave Town's first town meeting and election. The gathering was held in Bert Haskins' Mother Lode and was attended by all the business people, mine owners and other reputable citizens. Haskins was chosen mayor without a dissenting vote. Other officials were duly elected. Finally the important post of town marshal came up.

Bert Haskins rose to his feet. "Gents," he said, "town marshal is a mighty responsible job and we need a responsible man to fill it. In my opinion the man best fitted is Mort Lane."

There was a general voicing of agreement.

"But, Bert," Lane protested, "I haven't time to handle a marshal's chores properly. It's a twenty-four-hour-a-day job, and I'd be lucky if I could devote four to it. I just haven't the time to spare."

"Sure you haven't," Haskins agreed. "We know that, and nobody would expect you to handle the chores. You'll appoint a couple of deputies for that. But somebody with prestige and standing in the community should pack the authority. You're the man we need."

There were more shouts of agreement. Finally Lane reluctantly accepted the commission.

After due deliberation, two husky young miners, one of them a former cowhand, were selected as deputies. Lane held a conference with them.

"You don't want to pay much attention to small ruckuses and horse play," he said. "Things like that are to be expected. You can't expect the boys, with redeye buzzing in their ears, to behave like a Sunday school. What I want to prevent is serious trouble, bad gun play, and the like. Try and stop such things before they start. It's easier that way. Most Texans are law-abiding folks and respect authority. Don't go around with a chip on your shoulder, but when you give an order, make it stick. I'll back you to the limit and so will the rest of the community. We're building a calaboose right away, and if gents get too rambunctious, spending a night in the cells will most likely cool them down. We don't intend to set up a blue-law community where nobody can have any fun, but we are going to try and make Grave Town a place where decent folks will want to come and live. We can do it if we stick together. In a strike town like this there is always an element that will try to take over, and they will do it if they aren't stopped short. It's happened in other places and can happen here if we let them get the upper hand. We'll draw up a code of ordinances and we'll expect to have them obeyed. Crooked games in the saloons are out — that's a prime trouble maker — and caution the bar owners to keep an eye on gents who have swallowed all they can hold and ease up on them. It'll pay them in the end. I expect you'll find more to do down in the lower town than up here on the mesa. Okay, you've got your orders."

Later, Webb remarked to Lane, "Notice that Jess Rader and several more of the saloon and dance hall boys of the lower town weren't at the meeting."

"So I noticed," Lane replied. " 'Pears they didn't want to have any part of it. Not a good sign, either; I'm afraid we'll have trouble with them sooner or later. I've a notion Rader has ideas about running things down there. We'll have to keep an eye on him."

Webb nodded sober agreement. "That new feller Mike Day was there," he added. "Somebody pointed him out to me. Fine-looking jigger, isn't he? Makes me think of a duke or an earl — or what I've always figured a duke or an earl ought to look like. I never saw one."

"Chances are you'd be disappointed if you did," Lane returned. "They're just like other folks. But Day looks the way a nobleman should, and he seems to be all wool and a yard wide, too. He reminds me of somebody I've seen, or maybe a picture of somebody; I can't recall who."

"Maybe he's a duke or earl in disguise," hazarded Webb.

"Or a Spanish *hidalgo*," laughed Lane. "Could be; they had some in Nevada and California during the silver and gold rush days. Anyhow, that dancing girl who lives with him sure measures up to everything a princess should be," he added with conviction. "Pretty as a spotted pony, and she's got a hair-trigger mind. The way she handled that gun-slinging cowhand! Gentlemen, hush!"

"And from what you told me of the shindig, if it hadn't been for her, you might not be here right now," Webb remarked.

"You're right about that," Lane agreed soberly. "At any rate, she prevented what could easily have been a bad shooting. Even if he hadn't gotten me with the first shot, I'd have had to throw down on him."

"And I've noticed when you throw down on something, you don't miss," Webb observed. "And the others would have took it up and there would have been the devil to pay, even though it would have been plain that you shot in self-defence."

"Think I'd better drop in and really thank her right," Lane said. "I didn't have much chance last night."

"Do that," urged Webb. "Think I'll drop in, too; I'd like to have a look at her, and I've sort've took a shine to that Day feller. We could use more of his sort hereabouts, and less of the Rader brand."

Lane didn't argue that point, either; he, too, felt that they were getting a bit too many of the Rader type.

"Suppose we ride to Mike's place tonight?" Webb suggested. "It ain't late."

"Okay by me," Lane agreed. "Let's go."

Outside the Occidental, they tied their horses at a convenient rack and entered the saloon. Lane glanced about.

"There she is, sitting alone at that corner table," he said in low tones.

Old Andy followed the direction of his gaze and whistled under his breath. "She's something!" he enthused. "Oh, to be fifty again! Go on over and speak to her. I see Mike at the end of the bar; I'm going to have a talk with him."

Lane crossed to the corner table. The little dancer smiled at him.

"Hello!" she said warmly. "Won't you sit down?"

"Be plumb pleased to," he accepted, drawing up a chair. "You're not dancing to-night?" with a glance at her very becoming dress which, while short-skirted and cut low, was certainly not a dancing costume.

"No," she said, regretfully, "*he* prefers I don't dance any more, and of course, I wouldn't think of doing anything that would displease him." She nodded toward where Mike Day stood at the end of the bar.

Lane nodded. "You rather like Mike Day, don't you?" he couldn't resist asking.

"Yes," she replied, "very, very much." Lane thought there was an amused look in the big eyes as she said it, and wondered why.

"Mind telling me your name?" he said hesitantly.

"Of course not," she replied; "it's Mary. And you don't need to introduce yourself —

everybody knows you. You're Mr. Lane."

"Guess that's right," he admitted, "but — Mary, my friends usually call me Mort."

She laughed, a low, silvery laugh that reminded him of distant chiming bells over still water at night. "Okay — Mort," she said, a dimple at one corner enhancing the scarlet witchery of her mouth. "And that nice old gentleman who came in with you is Mr. Webb, is it not?"

"Yes, that's Andy, my partner," Lane answered. "He wanted to get a look at you and to have a talk with Mike. He saw him at the meeting this evening and liked him."

"He's easy to like, very easy to like," she said, glancing affectionately toward the end of the bar.

Mort Lane experienced a vague sense of "missing something." It must be nice to be liked that way. For no apparent good reason, he suddenly felt lonely.

She seemed to sense what was going through his mind, for her smile was abruptly very warm and understanding.

"Would you care to dance?" she asked. "He doesn't mind me dancing with people he approves of. After all, sitting around all night with nothing to do gets tiresome; but it's better than being alone in our cabin."

They danced together; admiring glances

followed them across the floor.

"They make just about the finest-looking couple I ever saw," old Andy Webb declared with conviction.

"I agree with you, heartily," said Mike Day. Mary and Lane returned to their table, the girl rosy and breathless.

"You're a good dancer," she complimented, "and very light on your feet for so big a man."

"Comes from scrambling around over the hills and rocks, I guess," Lane returned lightly. "If you don't learn to step right, you bust your neck."

He ordered drinks, whiskey for him and wine for her. She sipped her wine daintily.

"I don't drink much," she admitted, "only a little wine now and then."

"Your complexion shows that," he said.

"Thank you," she acknowledged the compliment. "Only I haven't been getting out in the sun enough of late; I'm losing my tan."

"Do you like to ride?" he asked, adding impulsively, "we have a couple of good horses in our stable."

"I love to," she replied.

"Okay, we'll take a ride together," he said. "How about day after tomorrow? Or would Mike object?"

"I'm sure he wouldn't," she answered, the

dimple back at the corner of her mouth.

She glanced toward the swinging doors as they opened. "Do you know that young man who just came in?" she asked.

Lane shook his head. "That jigger's so good-looking it hurts."

"Isn't he?" she said. "His features are cameo-perfect. Rather too much so for my taste. I prefer a man to look more rugged."

"Like Mike Day," he smiled.

"Yes," she said, "he has the famed beauty of the —" She didn't finish the sentence but said quickly, "That young man is the owner of the sheep ranch down to the south of here. His name is Barry Curtis and he's very nice. But I think he is rather lonely here in the cattle country."

"No reason for him to be," Lane said. "He's looking this way. Call him over; I'd like to meet him."

Mary beckoned to the newcomer, who walked hesitantly to the table, his glance on Lane's cowhand costume. Lane understood his diffidence and said cordially, "Take a load off your feet, Curtis. Mary just mentioned your name."

"Be glad to, if you don't mind sitting at the same table with a sheepman," he said with a grin.

"Well, I've sat at a table with sheep on it

and it never did me any harm," Lane smiled. "I've no objection to sheep, so long as they're handled right, and I understand yours are."

Curtis sat down and accepted a drink. "Yes, they are," he said. "My range is fenced and I move them from pasture to pasture. That way they do no damage to the grass."

Lane glanced at the other's hands and noted some scars and calluses that never came from shearing sheep.

"I've a notion you were a cowman once yourself," he observed.

"I was," Curtis admitted; "and with conditions as they've been for the past couple of years, I found I was slowly going broke. That's why I turned to sheep, as a lot of cowmen over in the Nueces and Trinity River country are doing. There's money in sheep. So I sold out and came over here and scouted around a bit. Decided the hilly range to the south of here would do fine. I learned it was state land and got title to a section. What I didn't learn was that somebody else was contemplating getting title; otherwise I'd have looked a bit farther. I'm afraid my neighbour to the south, John Bruton, is a bit on the prod against me."

"He'll get over it," Lane predicted cheerfully. "He's an old-timer and averse to prog-

139

ress, but when conditions change enough, even the old-timers find they have to go along."

"You know Bruton?" Curtis asked.

"Well, I met him once," Lane answered with a grin. "We didn't exactly agree, and I understand he sort of blames me for everything that's happened that doesn't suit him."

Curtis opened his eyes a bit. "Why, you must be Mort Lane!" he exclaimed.

"So I've always been told," Lane admitted.

"I intended to ride up and see you," Curtis said. "I thought maybe I could find a market up there for some of my surplus stock."

"Don't see any reason why you shouldn't," Lane replied. "Our rock busters live on whiskey and meat, and I wouldn't be surprised if quite a few of them like mutton. Suppose you ride up tomorrow evening. I'll meet you in The Mother Lode on Main Street, and we'll have a talk and I'll introduce you to some of our meat dealers. I've a notion they'll be glad to make a deal with you."

"I'll do that," Curtis said heartily, "and thank you very much. Well, think I'll drift over to the bar. I see a couple of my boys there. Be seeing you."

Mary smiled at Lane after the sheepman departed. "That was nice of you," she said. "I'm sure he appreciates it greatly. I still think he has been rather lonesome. And being lonesome isn't pleasant, as I have reason to know."

Lane glanced at her curiously, but she didn't choose to elaborate on her remark and he thought it best not to question her.

"I guess I'd better pick up Andy and be going, too," he said. "Got a busy day ahead of me tomorrow, and it's getting late. Thanks for the pleasure of the dance, and your company. I'll meet you here day after tomorrow at two for that ride."

"I'll be ready, Mort," she said. "Take care of yourself."

"And you take care of yourself," he answered. "All right; until day after tomorrow at two."

Andy and Day were absorbed in conversation when Lane approached them. The saloon-keeper greeted him courteously and warmly. "First chance I've had to thank you properly for what you did the other night," he said. "I think you prevented really serious trouble."

"I've a notion we have your Mary to thank for that," Lane returned. "If she hadn't whacked that cowboy, Pete Withrow, on the funny bone with her toe, there might have been powder burned, and that isn't good any place."

"I agree," Day replied. "It was the first thing like real trouble I've had since I took over here. I try to run a decent place."

"I'm sure you will," Lane told him. "And that's the sort of place we want. I'll tell my deputies to keep an eye on the place and be ready to lend you a hand if you should happen to need one. I doubt if you will, though; I've been looking over the crowd here and they all seem to be right jiggers."

As they rode back to the Mesa, old Andy observed, "I like that Day feller even better than I did at first; he's a real hombre."

"Learn anything about him?" Lane asked.

"Not much," Webb confessed. "He don't do much talking about himself, and in this country you don't ask questions."

Lane nodded agreement. "Chances are there isn't much to learn, anyhow."

"So I figure," said Webb. "But one thing is sure for certain; he knows how to pick girls."

"You can say that double," Lane agreed soberly.

"And you can't blame her for falling hard for him, even if he is a mite old," Webb added. "That jigger has got plenty!"

Lane soberly nodded agreement again.

CHAPTER XIV

The following afternoon, Lane met Helen Bruton on the range north of the trail, as he had promised he would. He found her in a humour bordering on bad temper.

"Dad and I had a grand row," she announced. "He was ranting about the sheep and mentioned your name. I told him I'd talked with you and that his estimate of you was all wrong. He went into the air for fair then, and it ended by me telling him he was an old fool and behind the times."

Lane was a bit shocked by this lack of parental respect but tried not to show it.

"What did he do?" he asked.

"Oh, he cooled down a bit after a while," she answered. "I told him I was going to ride up to Grave Town to do some shopping, that I'd heard I could get things in the stores there that I can't get in Buckley. He said all right and that he would send Sam Harness, our range boss, to ride back with me. Oh, I'll bring him around to my way of thinking sooner or later."

Lane wasn't so sure, but wisely did not argue the point.

It was nearly dark when they reached Grave Town. Lane accompanied her to the general stores, which were well stocked, and assisted her with her purchases.

"Sam will take care of packing them back to the spread," she said. "Let's get something to eat; I'm starved."

They repaired to The Mother Lode and enjoyed a good dinner. They were just ordering an after-dinner drink when Barry Curtis, the sheepman, came in and glanced about inquiringly. Lane caught his eye and beckoned him to their table.

"Helen, this is Barry Curtis," he said. "Reckon you've heard of him. Barry, this is Miss Bruton. Wouldn't be surprised if you've heard of *her*."

"Yes, I have," Curtis admitted as he acknowledged the introduction a trifle dazedly. Lane noticed that he had reddened to his hair.

He glanced at Helen. Her eyes were wide and there was a spot of colour in each creamily tanned cheek. He wondered if she was going to light into Curtis about the sheep.

She didn't. She merely smiled and said in her cool, pleasant voice, "Won't you sit down and join us in a drink, Mr. Curtis?"

The sheepman sat down a bit diffidently; Lane shared his evident perturbation.

But Helen sat serene, the eternal feminine of all the ages. Her conversation flowed pleasantly and she apparently did not notice the discomfort of the two males; and she very quickly had both at their ease. But Lane noticed that Curtis still flushed a little when she addressed him directly, and his answers were distrait.

It gradually dawned on Mort Lane that Mr. Curtis was badly smitten. The discovery amused him no little. He felt he ought to experience a certain resentment, but somehow he didn't, and wondered why.

The table was relaxed and animated when Sam Harness showed up. He did not appear the least surprised at the company in which he found old John's daughter. Lane wondered if anything ever surprised him and doubted if anything ever did.

Harness acknowledged the introductions, accepted a drink and rolled a cigarette. He grinned at Lane, and very soon they were discussing the mining and cattle business, Harness being well versed in the details of both.

"Got a bit of information for you, Lane,"

he announced after a while. "The Running W spread over to the east of the Coronado is for sale."

"What makes you think I'd be interested?" Lane asked.

Harness chuckled. "Once a cowman, always a cowman," he said. "After a while you'll get tired of grubbing among the rocks and will want to cast your eye on some mossy-backs for a change. It's a good holding and you can get it cheap. Old Wes Livesay who owns it lost his wife about a year back, and his daughter has been urging him to sell out and come over to the Brazos country and live with her. Wes finally decided he would. Reckon that big ranch-house gets lonesome for him nowadays. You ought to ride across and look the spread over."

"I've a notion maybe I will," Lane replied thoughtfully. He glanced at Helen as he spoke, but she was absorbed in conversation with Curtis and apparently had taken no note of what was said.

Harness looked at the clock behind the bar. "Helen, reckon we'd better be going," he said. "It's late."

"Yes, I suppose we'll have to," she replied, reluctantly, Lane thought. "Be seeing you, Mort. And I hope I'll see you again, too, Mr. Curtis."

146

"I certainly hope so," Curtis replied fervently.

After Helen and the range boss had taken their leave, Curtis turned to Lane, his eyes thoughtful.

"I've a notion," he said, "that she's not much like the old man."

"And I've a notion," Lane replied grimly, "that you'll find she's a lot more so than you think."

Lane introduced Curtis to a couple of merchants who came in and left them to discuss business matters. As he sat smoking, Bert Haskins joined him.

"See you're getting along okay with half the Bruton family, anyhow," he remarked as he sat down.

"And I hope eventually to get along with the other half, too," Lane replied.

"If you've got Helen on your side, you will," Haskins predicted. "I was a mite surprised when you walked in together, but not much. Helen always does just as she pleases. And she knows how to handle old John. He doesn't realise it, but she's been running the spread for the past few years. She knows more about the cattle business than he does. A tophand with a rope and a branding iron, too, and can she ride! She takes first prize at all the meets the spreads of the section hold after fall roundup. She backs the toughest outlaws they can bring in and gentles 'em. I don't believe there's a horse in Texas that can pitch her."

Lane gave him a puzzled look. "How about the big moros she rides?" he asked.

"Old Smoke, her pet saddle horse?" Haskins scoffed. "She could spread her blankets on Smoke's back and go to sleep there!"

Haskins lumbered off. Lane remained at the table, smoking, a pucker between his brows.

"But that moros *did* pitch her!" he muttered, adding uncertainly, "I saw him do it."

Mary was waiting at the door when Lane rode down to the Occidental the following afternoon, forking Rojo and leading Webb's sturdy roan. He gave her a glance of approval.

She wore plain Levi's that showed signs of much usage, a soft blue shirt, open at the throat, little scuffed riding boots, and a battered "J.B." perched jauntily on her black curls.

"Up you go!" he said, encircling her slender waist with his hands and lifting her lightly to the saddle.

"I don't believe you know how strong you are," she said breathlessly.

"What you don't realise is how small you are," he pointed out.

"I'm big enough."

"Doubtless."

She slanted a glance at him, coloured a little and laughed.

As they left the fringe of the town Lane said, "We'll head east, if you don't mind. Something over the other side of the Coronado Trail I want to take a look at, and I guess it doesn't make much difference which way we ride."

"None at all," she replied. "It's all so wonderful."

He glanced at her curiously. "And you don't find this country monotonous and tiresome after a while?"

The blue eyes turned to him wonderingly. "How could it ever become tiresome when it is so grand and free and beautiful?" she answered. "I love it! Oh, I've lived in cities and like them; but always, sooner or later, I get homesick for the rangeland. I'd never be content any place else. Why did you ask such a silly question?"

Lane was silent; he didn't know just how to answer, for he found it hard to explain to himself why he had asked.

After a while they crossed the broad Coronado Trail, fetlock deep in dust, and rode on. Soon they began passing clumps of cattle bearing the Running W brand. They were good-looking beefs, and Lane eyed them with appreciation. He also studied the terrain with a cowman's understanding. The buffalo grass was tall and heavy, and there were plenty of thickets and occasional groves. The hills to the north were slashed with canyons that promised shelter and shade. Several times they splashed through little streams.

Finally, as the sun was slanting well to the west, they sighted a big grey ranchhouse built Mexican style, advantageously placed on the crest of a low rise and surrounded by old trees. Barns, bunkhouse, corral and other outbuildings were tight and in good repair. Lane nodded approval of all he saw.

Gazing at the house, Mary exclaimed with pleasure, "What a beautiful old place! And those trees! I'd love to live there."

They were sitting their horses very close together as they spoke. Impulsively, Lane reached over and laid his hand on hers; she did not draw away. He thrilled to the warm contact but after a moment dropped his own hand.

"Sorry," he said. "I'm afraid Mike wouldn't like that." Mary turned to face him, and her eyes were crinkled at the corners.

"*Ojos que no yen, corazon que no ilora,*" she replied.

Lane looked puzzled. "I understand a good deal of Spanish, but I can't quite follow that," he admitted.

"It is a Spanish proverb, and means, 'If the eyes do not see, the heart does not grieve.'"

Lane shook his head. "That has a cynical twist, but the way you said it, it sounded like pure music," he said. "You don't speak Spanish like folks this side of the Border; it seems to come natural to you."

She hesitated before replying; then, "My father is of Spanish descent."

"And of the *hidalgo* type, I'm willing to bet," Lane declared with conviction.

"Well, one of his forebears was a Telo," she admitted.

Lane nodded without surprise. He had read of that great and noble family that for centuries was the bar on the northern gate of Spain. Suddenly he chuckled.

"Come to think of it, that's what Mike Day reminds me of more than anything else," he said. "A Spanish nobleman."

"Perhaps," Mary replied, the dimple showing at the corner of her red mouth, "but he's just a plain Texan."

"Well," Lane laughed, for he was an American, "I guess he can't aspire any higher than that."

Mary laughed with him, then glanced at the westering sun.

"Don't you think we'd better be going back?" she suggested. "It's growing late."

"Guess we had," he agreed. "Be dark before we reach town; I don't want Mike to think I've run away with you."

Mary smiled but did not otherwise reply.

It was dark when they reached the Occidental. Mike Day met them inside the door. He patted Mary's shoulder affectionately and gave Lane a cordial greeting.

"You must have dinner with us before you return to the mesa," he insisted. "I have the corner table laid with a cloth and silver."

"Be plumb glad to," Lane accepted the invitation. "I'm hungry as a steer after a hard winter."

He sauntered to the table and sat down. Mary lingered with Day, talking animatedly. Lane could see that her eyes were filled with laughter.

She seemed to be urging some course of which Day disapproved, for he shook his head in a bewildered fashion and appeared to expostulate with her. Finally, however, he threw out his hands in a gesture of resignation. Mary stood on tiptoe to kiss his bearded cheek and danced across to the table. Mort Lane suppressed a sigh.

As he rode up the winding trail to the mesa, Lane wondered what was the matter with him. He had not resented Barry Curtis' undoubted interest in Helen Bruton; but with no justification, he was beginning to resent Mike Day.

CHAPTER XV

Two days later Lane met Helen by the Buckley trail. As they rode across the range together, she made a suggestion.

"Suppose we go and look over the sheep ranch. I've never seen one."

"Suits me," Lane agreed. "Maybe we'll see Curtis: I like him."

Helen slanted him a sideways glance but said nothing. When they reached the wire in front of Curtis' ranch-house, Lane let out a shout. A moment later Curtis himself appeared in the door. He hurried to open the gate for them.

"This *is* a pleasant surprise," he exclaimed. "I'm glad to see you both. Come in! Come in!"

"Helen wanted to see the sheep," Lane explained.

"I'll be glad to show them to you, and everything," Curtis replied. "Wait till I get my horse."

They rode about the holding, while Curtis explained the working of the ranch. Lane was not particularly interested, but Helen was a rapt listener. After a while they rode back to the ranch-house and Curtis suggested they go in for coffee and cake. Helen instantly accepted the invitation.

Over the coffee and cake, the conversation about sheep and other things continued. Lane listened with considerable amusement, his thoughts wandering. It was two hours later when they left the ranch.

"He's certainly an interesting man," Helen observed as they waved goodbye to Curtis.

"And interested," Lane chuckled.

There was a peculiar expression in the blonde girl's eyes as she replied, "I suppose if one is born a fool it is only to be expected that one will remain a fool for the rest of one's days."

Lane hadn't the least notion what she meant and she didn't explain. He felt it was best not to ask questions.

They had just reached the Buckley Trail when they sighted a horseman riding from the south at a fast pace. A moment later Lane recognised John Bruton.

"Oh, Lord!" he exclaimed thoroughly disconcerted, "now we *are* in for it!"

"Don't worry," Helen replied coolly. "I'll handle him."

Old John reined in a few paces distant. His face was red, his moustache bristling.

"So!" he rumbled accusingly. "You've been meeting this young whippersnapper!"

"Yes, I have! What of it?" Helen snapped.

"What of it!" bawled old John. "I ought to take you over my knee!"

"You can't do it, and you know better than to try," his daughter retorted. "And I'm past twenty-one and don't have to take orders from you or anybody else."

Old John raised both fists above his head and said things he shouldn't.

"Oh, cool down!" Helen told him. "Do you always have to make a spectacle of yourself? I'll meet anybody I want to, any time I want to. And what's more, Mort's coming home to dinner with us."

"What!" bellowed Bruton.

"You heard what I said."

Old John appeared about to explode. Lane tried hard to look serious, but Bruton's scandalised amazement was so comical that he had to grin.

Bruton glared; then suddenly he grinned, too. And abruptly his bad-tempered old face was wonderfully pleasing and youthful.

"Son," he said in conversational tones,

"don't ever get married. See what you'll have to put up with!"

"I expect he'd be able to stand it," Helen said. "Let's go!"

After a really excellent dinner, Mort Lane sat in the big living room with Bruton, and they found they had plenty to talk about. Helen sat a little apart, idly turning the pages of a book and taking small part in the conversation; her thoughts seemed to be elsewhere.

The talk finally got around to sheep and the sheep ranch. "I don't know what the country's coming to!" Bruton declared. "I thought barbed wire was bad enough, but sheep!"

"Mr. Bruton," Lane said, "I'm going to suggest something with which you may not agree, but which I think it would pay you to give some thought to. You have a lot of hill pasture that isn't much good for cows but which would be prime for sheep."

"Sheep!" snorted old John. "*Me* raise sheep?"

"There's a limit to the losses even a big rancher can take," Lane replied significantly. "There's money in sheep, and over east a lot of spread owners, with the cattle market what it is, are turning to them. There's no use trying to stop the wheels of progress, sir. Times are changing, and the only thing to do is to change with them. When you see something that is to your advantage, even though it conflicts with preconceived notions, take advantage of it."

Old John snorted again, but he tugged his moustache and looked thoughtful.

After Lane had said goodnight, old John turned to his daughter.

"That young jigger is considerable more of a feller than I would have suspected," he observed.

"Yes, I suppose he is," Helen agreed absently.

Lane had a talk with Walt Slaven, his agent. The result of the talk was the purchase of the Running W spread. Slaven approved warmly.

"It's a good investment," he declared. "Some day the gold ledges may peter out, but people will still have to eat, and there'll always be an income for a man who has cattle to sell."

"That's the way I feel about it," Lane agreed. "While I have the money, I might as well invest it in something that will last."

He did not tell Slaven — in fact he didn't even admit to himself — that what had really made him decide to buy the Running W was the remark made by Mary that she'd love to live in the old Livesay ranch-house.

Grave Town was still growing. The school was nearly completed, another stamp mill was being built, and a group of pious citizens were erecting a church, of which Lane heartily approved. The shacks and cabins were being replaced by substantial homes. There were new general stores, and specialty shops were appearing on Main Street.

East of the Coronado Trail, surveyors were running lines, gangs were levelling and grading, and the steel fingers of the railroad were inching westward. One day a group of well dressed, keen-eyed men paid a visit to Mort Lane.

"We represent the C. & P. Railroad, Mr. Lane," they told him. "We want to build an assembling yard, shops and a roundhouse just east of your town. We understand you own the land, and we're here to do business with you."

"Don't see any reason why we can't come to terms, " Lane replied. "We want the railroad to come through here and are glad to cooperate."

A satisfactory arrangement was arrived at, and soon the barren ground south and east of the mesa was a scene of busy activity.

Mort Lane was seeing the realisation of his dream of two years before when he had looked across the barren mesa and envisioned — instead of sage and mesquite — a town.

He enjoyed the friendship of old John, and Mort was the only person in the section who wasn't astounded when the word got around that Bruton was fencing a section of his hill pastures and was bringing in sheep.

"You see, I took your advice," the rancher told Lane. "I hated to do it, but I'll have to admit I've lost more money in the past two years than I can afford. Maybe the sheep will pull me out of it. I hired some fellers who know the business to look after them. They don't seem such a bad sort."

"The chances are you'll find them not much different from cowhands," Lane predicted. "Folks are generally about the same, no matter what line they're in. There are good ones and bad ones, and that's about the only difference."

"I've a notion maybe you're right," Bruton admitted. Lane tried to stay away from the Occidental, but he couldn't. Mary was always glad to see him and they got along fine together. Lane was careful, however, to keep the conversation on a gay and impersonal basis. Sometimes he would

160

catch a mocking light in the blue eyes that filled him with a vague uneasiness; he couldn't explain just why.

Mike Day was also always cordial and apparently harboured no resentment over his being in the girl's company so much. This puzzled Lane; it didn't seem natural.

CHAPTER XVI

One night Lane hesitantly made a suggestion. "Been quite a while since we took our last ride," he observed. "What say we take another one tomorrow, over to the west and around through the lower hills? I've a notion it would be interesting. We can start early in the morning, if it's all right with you, pack some chuck and some coffee and sort of camp out."

"I'd love it," she instantly replied. "I can be ready as early as you are. I'll meet you in front of the place."

"Okay," he said, "an hour after sunup."

They rode out of town as the level rays of the rising sun burned the grassheads with dew fire that a little breeze shook down in a myriad of sparkling gems. Larks sang in the golden glow and there was a whisper of autumn cold in the shadowy hollows. For several miles they rode due west, then turned north. Ahead, blue-purple in the distance, loomed the sprawling spurs shooting off from the main body of Espantosa Hills, their naked slopes scored with gloomy canyons and dry washes walled in by frowning cliffs. The jagged crests raked the blue curve of the sky, jutting up like snaggly teeth in a bleached jawbone.

They were ugly, those grim hills, but paradoxically beautiful with the stark, elemental beauty of the wastelands. The sun was just beginning to climb the long eastern slants of the heavens, and their bleak outlines were softened by the elusive dregs of shadow that were already tipped with glowing saffron.

A grey monotony the broken slopes seemed from a distance; but as they drew nearer they saw that the cliffs walling the canyons were bright with colour. There were raw, metallic reds, dusky wines, vivid greens and strange, beautiful mouse shades merging with ruddy bronze, dusty cinnamon and pale amber, with here and there the leprous white of borax outcroppings.

Those rainbow-hued cliffs interested Mort Lane. "Gold and silver aren't the only valuable metals," he explained to Mary. "Those rusty red splotches may indicate iron; the velvety reds could very well be outcroppings of cinnabar ore — that's what you get quicksilver from — and the greens might mean only vegetable matter stains, and then again they might mean copper. Something to keep in mind if the gold ledges should take a notion to peter out some day. This country has everything needed to make people prosperous and happy, if they'll only work for it."

"And it's a pleasure to work and plan and hope amid such beauty," she replied softly, her eyes dreamy. Lane glanced at her elfinly beautiful little face and sighed.

About noon they rode into a rather narrow canyon with sloping, rocky sides. Or, rather, it was a trough between two mountain slopes. They left their horses and scrambled up a dim, zigzag trail that was but a game track winding between the boulders and clumps of mesquite. Finally, breathless, they paused at the base of a round, bare peak of jagged bronze stone nearly half a mile above the canyon floor. Seated comfortably with their backs to the rock, they gazed onto a stupendous view that flowed into the infinity of the west.

"Look!" Mary suddenly exclaimed. "An eagle!"

Entranced, they gazed at the great lonely bird perched on a pinnacle on the far side of the canyon. And even as they gazed, the eagle pitched from the crag and spread its mighty wings. Up and up it rose, in a great circle, drawing ever nearer until it was less than fifty feet below them. Another moment and they could clearly see the wonderful clean-cut head and the cruel beak, and even the flash of wild, untamed eyes. Higher and higher, with never a movement of the great wings. Now it was above them, its shadow falling across their upturned faces. Then the winds of the upper heights caught him, ruffling his feathers. Magnificently he breasted them, then swooped like a falling star across the heavens, a flame of bronze and gold merging with the blue of the sky, and was gone. The two watchers sat silent, awed by this miracle of the sun and the wind and the blue immensities. A handspan of eternity imprisoned in a bird!

Lane became aware that Mary was gazing at him. She breathed deeply and said in a low voice:

"Shall we be going? There may be more wonders for us still to find."

As they descended to the canyon floor, Lane glanced about and spied a trickle of water seeping from beneath a cliff.

"Plenty of wood hereabouts," he said. "Suppose we boil a bucket of coffee and have a bite to hold us over till supper time?"

"Fine!" the girl agreed. She moved to the

edge of the growth and began breaking twigs and peeling bits of tinder-dry bark.

"Give me your matches and I'll get the fire started while you open the pack," she said.

Lane handed her a flat, tightly-corked bottle, the cowboy's waterproof container, and Mary got the fire going.

It was close to sunset and the sky was a riot of scarlet and gold when they entered another canyon, in search of a suitable spot to make camp and cook supper. It was narrow, well-grassed and dotted with clumps of chaparral. A little distance inside the gorge, they found a spring of cool water with straggles of dry growth on either side.

"This will do fine," Lane remarked, dismounting. He glanced up the canyon and his brows drew together in perplexity. A couple of hundred yards distant was a belt of tall thick growth, and from beyond the growth rose feathery plumes of mist.

"Now what the devil?" he wondered. "Let's go see."

They pushed their way through the growth and found themselves on the bank of a pool a dozen yards or so in diameter. The bottom was clean white sand and sloped so that the lower end of the pool was a good six feet in depth, the upper only a few inches.

All around the mesquite was green and brown. Occasional cottonwoods had begun to change from green to amber and bronze. From the surface of the pool rose wisps of vapour.

"Well, I'll be darned!" exclaimed Lane. "A hot spring! And that's a good sign of mineral in the rocks, too."

Mary knelt and dipped her hand in the water. "It's deliciously warm," she said, and began drawing off her boots.

"I'm going to stop here and bathe my feet in it," she added. "You go ahead and get the camp started; I'll be with you shortly."

"Okay," Lane agreed. "Take your time — there's no hurry. Will take me a bit to get things going."

He left her and returned to the spring of cool water, whistling. He got the rigs off the horses and turned them loose to graze. Then he opened the pack, spread out the provisions and cooking utensils and gathered wood for a fire.

CHAPTER XVII

Lane was concerned over conditions in the lower town, and so was Webb.

"We're getting a regular 'South of the Tracks' like they had in Dodge City," declared old Andy. "Jess Rader and the bunch that strings along with him are complaining that the regulations hurt business. Mort, I tell you they're getting together and aim to make trouble. I figure they're planning to take over, pull away and form a town government of their own that will allow them to do as they please."

"They can't do that," Lane replied. "I've got a club to hold over them; I can close them up any time I'm of a mind to. In every lease there is a stipulation that if, in my judgment, a place isn't conducted in the best interests of Grave Town, I can terminate the lease at once. Judge Arbaugh drew up those leases, and they're air-tight."

"But just the same, they can make a heck

of a lot of trouble," Webb predicted. "I don't like it. And speaking of Judge Arbaugh, I was talking to him last week, and he wants to know when we're going to locate our *amigo* Pedro Lopez, or Miguel de Alba, which evidently is his right handle. The Judge says the money to his credit is piling up till it bothers him."

"I know it," Lane agreed, "but the jigger seems to have evaporated in thin air. The only thing pertaining to him that I've been able to learn is that he had a daughter living in El Paso with her mother's people. About three years ago she packed up and left, presumably to join de Alba, her father. Then *she* dropped out of sight. But we'll keep on looking. Surely somebody will have a line on where he is. Of course he's sort of in hiding, figuring the Rangers are on the lookout for him over the McMullen trouble, but he can't stay undercover forever. I'll write some more letters."

Lane's fears concerning real trouble in the lower town were not unfounded. There was a vicious fight in Jess Rader's First Chance, in the course of which a man was knifed to death by one of Rader's dealers. The dealer headed for parts unknown before the deputies could close in on him.

When Lane heard about the killing, which came close to being a cold-blooded murder, his face was bleak. He immediately rode to the First Chance and confronted Rader.

"This is my final warning," he told the saloon-keeper. "One more occurrence like what happened here last night and you're out."

Rader's face grew ugly. "Lane," he said, "sometime you'll go too far. You'll stick your nose into my affairs once too often."

"Yes, once too often," Lane told him. "After that you won't have any affairs, not in this town. And if you're looking for trouble, I'll fill you so full of it it'll run out of your ears."

He paused, looking Rader full in the eye, his hands swinging loosely at his sides.

For a moment, Rader's unwinking black eyes met the marshal's cold gaze. Then he glanced aside, muttered something under his breath and slouched away. Lane turned his back on him and walked from the saloon. As he went out he heard a voice remark:

"Jess had better listen to good advice and not go looking for any trouble; that feller sure aims to be accommodating."

Nevertheless, Mort Lane did not underestimate Rader and his trouble-making potentialities. Rader had a following, a

170

following that was constantly being augmented by new arrivals. The booming prosperity of Grave Town was attracting newcomers from all over the Southwest and elsewhere, not all of them desirable.

Stern old Sheriff McDonald rode up from Buckley and gave Rader a blistering tongue-lashing. Then he visited Mort Lane.

"A pity you couldn't drop a loop on that knifer," he said. "Looks like you might have been able to run him down."

"Yes, maybe we could have," Lane replied, "only we don't pack any authority outside the town limits. It would have been taking the law in our own hands, which isn't good."

"That's just what I want to talk to you about," said the sheriff. "I aim to speak to the county commissioners and get them to authorise me to swear you in as a deputy sheriff in charge up here. That'll give you all the authority you need to handle any trouble."

Lane debated the proposition a moment. "Well, okay," he agreed at last, reluctantly. "Seems I'm getting mixed up in the peace officer business, something I had no intention of doing, but perhaps it's a good notion."

"I think it is," replied the sheriff. "It will

give you some real authority. Your standing right now as marshal of this town that has never really been properly organised under state law is a bit dubious. As a deputy sheriff of the county, you'll be packing all the authority you're likely to need."

A few nights later Lane was in the Occidental, sitting at the table with Mary, when he saw Jess Rader push through the swinging doors and glance about.

"Come in to see how business is with his competitor, the chances are," Lane mused.

After hesitating a moment, Rader sauntered down the bar to where Mike Day was standing. Lane watched him idly. Day voiced a courteous greeting to which Rader did not immediately reply. He stood with his opaque eyes fixed on Day's face. Then he leaned close and spoke a few sentences in a low tone.

The effect on Day was startling. He stepped back, his eyes widening. It seemed to Lane that his face paled and that he was at a loss how to answer whatever it was Rader had said. Before he could recover his composure, Rader grinned, or rather his sunken face went through a contortion doubtless intended for a grin. Then he turned on his heel and left the saloon, looking neither to right nor left. Mike Day stared after him, seemingly dazed. Then he walked slowly to the back room and closed the door behind him.

"Now what did that snake-eyed devil say to Mike that upset him so?" Lane wondered. "He looked like he'd seen a ghost."

He was glad that Mary, whose back was to the bar, had not noticed the incident, and he was pondering Day's peculiar behaviour when her voice broke in on his thoughts.

"Mort," she said, "what's the matter? You aren't paying a bit of attention to what I'm saying."

"Yes I am, honey," he replied, coming back to his immediate surroundings with a start. "I heard every word you said; I was just looking things over."

"I suppose that is in line with your job as marshal," she admitted.

Lane went on with their conversation, but he was still puzzled over Mike Day's reaction to whatever it was Jess Rader had said to him. However, when Day came out of the back room a few minutes later, he walked over to the table and greeted Lane with his usual cordiality and made no mention of Rader.

But it seemed to Lane that his face was a bit haggard and that there was a worried look in the fine dark eyes.

One evening, about a week after the puzzling incident in the Occidental, the two deputies came hurrying into the marshal's office in the front of the new jail, where Lane happened to be at the moment. Concern was written large on their faces.

"Boss," one exclaimed without preamble, "Jack Richardson is in town!"

"That so?" Lane replied. "And who is Jack Richardson?"

"You mean to say you never heard of him?" the deputy asked incredulously. "He's just about the coldest killer this end of Texas ever saw. I reckon he's killed a dozen men, more or less, always in 'self-defence.' His play is to rile the other jigger into reaching first. Richardson waits till he gets hold of his gun handle and then pulls and kills him. I don't believe there's a man in Texas who can shade him on the draw."

"Sounds like an unsavoury character, all right," Lane admitted. "But if he's dropped in town for a mite of diversion, I don't see how we can very well ask him to leave, so long as he behaves himself."

"Boss," the deputy replied sententiously, "I don't think Richardson just dropped in, and I don't think he's here looking for diversion. I believe he was brought in and is here on business."

"Yes?" Lane was still not particularly impressed. "Who brought him in, and for what business?"

"I believe," the deputy replied, "that Jess Rader and his bunch sent for him — Richardson's gun is always for hire — and I believe his business here is to kill you."

"Sure you aren't imagining all this, Pete?" Lane asked a bit incredulously.

"No, I'm not!" the deputy declared vigorously. "I believe that's just his game."

Lane began rolling a cigarette. "You could be right," he admitted thoughtfully. "It sounds like Rader. Where's Richardson now — in Rader's place?"

"No," the deputy said. "Rader's too smart for that. Richardson is in the Occidental; everybody knows you drop in there 'most every night. He's got a couple of hellions with him that look as bad as he is and who will be all set to swear that you reached first and Richardson had to shoot in self-defence."

Lane lighted the cigarette. "Well," he said, "guess I'll drop into the Occidental tonight."

"Okay," Pete replied, hitching his gun belt a little higher. "Let's go."

Lane shook his head. "No, you and Clem

175

are staying right here," he vetoed the suggestion. "If I can't handle this business by myself, I'd better turn in my badge."

He drew the badge from his pocket as he spoke and pinned it on his shirt front.

"Boss, don't do it," Pete pleaded earnestly. "Richardson is waiting for you. He'll taunt you into reaching and then he'll down you. I tell you he's got the fastest gunhand in the Southwest. You're good, I ain't saying you ain't, but you won't have a chance with him."

"Other things besides fast gunhands," Lane observed, still apparently not much impressed.

"But there's three of the sidewinders," broke in Clem. "Let us go along and make things even."

"I think it'll be better for me to go alone for just that reason," Lane replied. "There's not much chance they'll all three jump me at once. That would show premeditation, and such a killing would be looked on as cold-blooded murder. Then they'd have the Rangers after them, and no matter how salty a jigger is, that's something he doesn't hanker for. Going up against the Texas Rangers is just slow suicide. Yes, I think I'll do better by myself. And maybe you're wrong about the whole business, and if we all go barging in there together, it might provoke trouble where none was intended."

"I hope to heaven you're right," answered Pete, his voice shaking a little. "But don't forget, Jack Richardson is the kind of gunslinger who has an itch to kill."

Lane stood up, grinned at the perturbed pair and went to get his horse.

When Lane entered the Occidental he noticed two things out of the ordinary. Mary was not at the corner table, and Mike Day was behind the bar, polishing glasses. Also, he sensed an air of tenseness that was unusual to the place.

Lane had no trouble spotting Jack Richardson. He was sitting at a nearby table with two companions. He had a face that was corpse-like in its pallor, a pallor accentuated by the blackness of lank hair worn so long it almost swept his coat collar. His eyes were also so pale as to make the sockets appear empty. But in their depths was a cold glitter, like dagger points in the sun. He was powerfully built, with abnormally long arms ending in long bony hands that resembled spear points as they hung limply by his sides.

All this Mort Lane saw in one swift, all-embracing glance. Without paying further attention to the unsavoury trio, he sauntered to the bar, tossed a greeting to Day and ordered a drink. He was not in the least surprised when a hand touched his shoulder. He knew that Richardson had risen from his table by the hush that suddenly fell over the room. He turned slowly to face the killer.

Before speaking, Richardson looked Lane up and down. His voice was like the harsh rumble of a carnivorous beast when he finally opened his lips.

"Hmmm!" he remarked, his eyes fixed on the marshal's badge. "Understand you think you're considerable salty. Two guns and everything. Hmmm! From where *I* come from, salty hombres don't have to hide behind a tin plate!"

The result of the viciously offensive remark was explosive, instant and utterly unexpected.

Lane did not reach for his gun, knowing well that he could never hope to equal, much less beat, Richardson's lightning draw. His left fist shot out and crashed against Richardson's jaw. As the killer reeled back half-dazed, pawing at his guns, Lane whipped his own Colt from its sheath and bent the barrel over Richardson's head. He went down, knocked senseless, blood pouring from his split scalp.

In the same move, Lane whirled sideways and around. From the tail of his eye he had seen Richardson's table companions come to their feet with a rush.

But even as he turned a voice spoke in pleasantly conversational tones.

"Be careful, gentlemen; this thing packs eleven buckshot to the cartridge, and it's got hair-triggers!"

Elbows resting on the bar, Mike Day stood with a sawed-off shotgun clamped against his shoulder. The twin black muzzles seemed to yawn hungrily at the pair at the table.

There had been the beginning of tumult, but now everybody sat or stood rigid; a scattergun has a habit of seeking out stray nooks and corners.

"You will raise your hands, shoulder high," said Mike, still pleasantly conversational. "So! Now you will be so kind as to turn around — slowly — and face the wall. Thank you!"

Subdued laughter ran around the room. Lane chuckled as he crossed to the motionless pair, careful to keep out of line with the shotgun.

"Thanks, Mike," he flung over his shoulder. He plucked the men's guns from their holsters and tossed them on the bar.

Running his hands over their bodies, he extracted still another gun from a shoulder holster and a knife from the back of a neck.

"Regular walking arsenals," he commented as the weapons joined the other hardware on the bar. "Stay put, you two."

He bent over the unconscious Richardson and removed his guns. He straightened up and glanced around the room.

"What say, Al?" he called to a man he knew. "Will you hitch up your light wagon and bring it around in front? These gents here are due for a ride up to the mesa, and that one on the floor doesn't seem to want to wake up."

"Be right with you, Mort." The man addressed chuckled and hurried from the room.

The prisoners were allowed to sit down till the wagon put in an appearance. Then Lane ordered them to carry Richardson out and lay him in the bed. They did so, glaring murderously but not hankering for a pistol whipping as the price of disobedience. They hunkered down beside him, and half a dozen witnesses to the affair piled in to keep them company. Lane mounted his horse, and the triumphal procession wound up the trail to the mesa, followed by cheers from the crowd that had poured out of the Occidental.

When they reached the new calaboose, the recently appointed jailer took charge. He was an old former cowboy whose badly broken and poorly set leg barred him from further range work; but his hands were as good as ever and he had seven notches filed on the butt of his old single-action Smith & Wesson.

"Lay the wind spider on the table there," he told the sullen bearers. "I'll patch him up. Had considerable experience at that sort of chore. All right, you two — in the cells!"

Half an hour later Jack Richardson, still dazed, his aching head swathed in bandages, staggered into a cell to mingle his curses with those of his companions. Very shortly afterward, the three crestfallen badmen were haled before Mayor Haskins, who held impromptu court in the marshal's office. After hearing the evidence, he at once sentenced them to six months for disturbing the peace.

"Richardson did just what I hoped and expected he would do," Lane explained to the mayor. "He walked up to me and got within arm's reach. He was all set to draw, but there's no man living who can pull a gun as fast as a man can hit with his fist. Richardson got what he least expected and wasn't prepared for — a solid punch on the jaw that knocked him off balance. Mike Day did a fine chore, though. He stopped what might have ended in a shooting. Cool as a frozen snake! You'd have thought he was asking those two killers to have a drink."

"You handled it plumb perfect," Haskins declared. "If you'd shot it out with them and downed all three it wouldn't have been half so good. You made Richardson look plumb silly. Everybody in town is laughing at him, and the story will spread all over Texas. Nobody will ever be scared of him again. I figure when he gets out his nerve will be busted, and I predict somebody will kill him inside of a year."

Big Val Jackson, owner of the Cross C, and his turbulent band were frequent Occidental visitors, and they always had a riotous greeting for Mort Lane.

"Why couldn't we have been here that night!" wailed Jackson. "We'd have left those hydrophobia skunks looking like so much barbecued beef! I see it plain, feller: we got to keep a better watch on you from now on."

Although he appreciated their solicitude, Lane was devoutly thankful the trigger-happy bunch hadn't been present the night of the Richardson incident. Without a doubt, there would have been a corpse-and-cartridge session for the next generation to talk about.

Meanwhile Mike Day had an unpleasant interview with Jess Rader.

"So you double-crossed me, eh?" said the First Chance owner, his death's-head face set in vindictive lines. "All right, you'll pay. I'm writing that letter."

"Go ahead and do your darnedest," Day told him. "I'm tired of it all, anyhow." He turned and walked away.

Rader gazed after him in baffled fury. He was a shrewd article and never allowed his emotions to sway his judgment unduly. He earnestly desired to wreak vengeance on Mike Day for the part he had played in the Richardson affair, but he had an uneasy premonition that if he did so, he might have to deal with Mort Lane on a personal basis, which he had no hankering to do. Rader was no coward, but he did not under-estimate an adversary. The marshal of Grave Town was a cold proposition.

When Mary saw Lane, her reaction was much the same as Val Jackson's.

"I wish I'd been there," she said, her eyes flashing. "I'd have shown that killer how I can kick when I really mean it.

"I might have known something was in the wind," she added. "My — Mike saw to it that I had a chore to do in the cabin that kept me busy all evening."

"He was absolutely right," Lane replied soberly. "No sense in exposing you to danger."

Mary looked decidedly unconvinced.

Jack Richardson's ludicrous debacle had a salutary effect on other badmen. They decided Grave Town was not a good place to coil their twine.

"That blamed pueblo's too well named," one declared morosely. "Go fooling around there and you're liable to take up permanent residence — on Boothill!"

CHAPTER XVIII

"We're getting plumb respectable," declared Andy Webb. He chuckled as a mellow clang sounded on the evening air.

"Hear that?" he said. "That's the new church bell, calling folks to prayer meeting. Son, when you looked across the mesa that morning you sure 'saw' something! You ought to be mighty happy over how things have worked out."

"Yes, I suppose I should," Lane returned moodily.

Old Andy shot him a searching glance. "What's the matter?" he asked. "Is it that Bruton gal? By the way, I saw her yesterday, down on the Buckley trail. She was out riding with that young sheep-raising feller, Barry Curtis."

"The devil you did!" Lane exclaimed.

"That's right," Webb replied. "And they sure made a purty couple. I don't think I ever saw two nicer-looking people."

"And I doubt if you ever will," Lane agreed. To himself he repeated a remark he made once before:

"Uh-huh, it looks like I'm left outside the corral altogether."

He would have been even more sure could he have overheard a conversation that took place that very night between John Bruton and his daughter.

"Dad," Helen asked, "you wouldn't want me to run away with a man, would you?"

"No, I wouldn't," answered old John. "But I wouldn't put it past you to do just that; you're plumb capable of it."

"Yes, I guess I am," Helen agreed. "So don't you think it will be better for you to give your consent and blessing?"

"Who is it?" Bruton asked. "That young feller Mort Lane? I sure ain't got any objection to him."

"No, it isn't Mort," she replied. "I like Mort, but he and I would never hit it off. He'd want to do one thing and I'd want to do another, and I don't like him well enough to be satisfied with what *he* wants. It's Barry Curtis."

"That sheepherder!" old John exploded.

"Well, we've already got sheep in the family, so I don't see how a sheepherder can hurt much," Helen returned composedly.

"Besides, if I marry him I'll be staying here with you. If I married Mort Lane, I'd finally tease him into taking me to a city to live. But with Barry, I'll be content to live even in this country. So what do you say? Do we get your consent, or will we have to do it without?"

Bruton threw out his hands. "Oh, what's the use arguing with you!" he snorted. "You always get your way. Good Lord! What's the world coming to! I think I'll go out and marry a squaw."

"Might be a good thing," his daughter admitted. "When you got to raring and charging, she'd bend a skillet over your head."

It was a few days later that Mort Lane made his great discovery.

He was standing in front of The Mother Lode when he saw Mike Day and Mary walking on the opposite side of the street, their arms linked affectionately. They paused before a shop window, and something they saw appeared to amuse them greatly, for they laughed aloud, looking into each other's eyes.

And the laugh of the one was the echo of the laugh of the other!

Mort Lane stared, his jaw sagging.

"Well, I'll be —" he sputtered. "Of all the

187

dumb yearlings I'm the dumbest! Nose the same! Mouth the same! Eyes different colour but shaped exactly the same! Hair the same, only Mike's has grey in it and hers hasn't! Same way of holding their heads! Same way of moving their hands! Same smile! Why in blazes didn't I tumble to it before? That little devil! Will I get even with *her* before everything's finished!"

He whirled about and fairly plunged into the Mother Lode for a drink; he felt he needed it!

That night he walked into the Occidental, sat down opposite Mary and without preamble shot a question at her:

"Mary, just what is Mike Day to you, anyhow?"

The blue eyes were brimful of laughter and mischief as she replied:

"Mort, you're making a joke with me. You know very well that Mike Day is my father!"

"But why in the devil didn't you tell me in the first place?" Lane exploded.

"Well," she replied demurely, "as I recall, you never asked me."

The roguish dimple showed at the corner of her mouth. "Oh, I knew what you were thinking, and I got a lot of fun out of it," she added. "I decided to keep up the joke for a while and string you along. Dad thought I was being terrible, but I teased him into promising not to say anything. It's lucky for you you didn't do any subtle probing or I would have led you a merry dance. 'Better to be an old man's darling than a young man's slave,' and so forth."

Lane regarded her gloomily. "You imp of Satan!" he said. "What I should do is turn you over my knee!"

The dimple appeared again, and was accompanied by a giggle.

Looking at her, Mort Lane admitted what heretofore he had refused to admit to himself: that he wanted this small, big-eyed girl more than all the rest of the world put together.

"Mary," he said, "will you marry me?"

There was nothing coy about Mary Day. She was straightforward and sincere.

"Yes, Mort, I will," she replied, "if my father will consent."

"I don't think there'll be any trouble in that quarter," Lane said cheerfully. "I've a notion he rather likes me."

"He does, more than you know, but there may be something that will cause him to hesitate," she said, and Lane saw there was pain in the blue eyes, and a hint of tears.

It puzzled him a little, but he was too thoroughly happy and too altogether in love to give much heed to what he put down as mere girlish anxiety, perhaps a fear that her father might not want to lose her. He began to talk animatedly about their future and the plans he had for both of them. That night, for the first time, he walked with her to the neat little cabin and kissed her goodnight.

"I'll see your dad around noon tomorrow, as soon as he shows up at the place," he told her. "Don't worry, honey; everything will be all right."

"I hope so," she answered, clinging to him. "Take care of yourself, my darling, and good luck!"

CHAPTER XIX

The following day Lane was at the Occidental promptly at noon. There was nobody around but Mike Day and a bartender who was eating his breakfast at a table at the other side of the room. Lane wasted no time.

"Mike," Lane said, "I want to ask a big favour of you."

"It is already granted — anything within my power," Day instantly responded.

"Mike," Lane said, "I want to marry your daughter. It's okay with her if you'll give your consent."

Day did not appear particularly surprised, but he slowly shook his head.

"Lane," he said, "I greatly regret that I cannot give my consent."

Mort Lane was decidedly taken aback. "But why not?" he asked. "I know I'm not good enough for her, but really, I'm not so terribly bad, am I?"

"You are one of the finest young men I

have ever known," Day replied. "And it is because of my high regard for you that I cannot consent to an alliance that will bring you trouble and disgrace."

"Doesn't seem to make sense to me," Lane differed, "but would you mind telling me what you mean?"

"I might as well," Day answered wearily; "you'll learn about it soon enough, anyway. Lane, I'm a fugitive from justice!"

"That so?" Lane said. "What did you do to get the law after you?"

"I killed a man."

Lane was not impressed. "Well," he replied cheerfully, "knowing you as I do, I figure he must have had a killing coming."

"He did have," Day returned grimly. "But just the same I fear I must pay for the deed with a term of imprisonment. I was arrested for the shooting, which took place in the course of a card game, and taken back for trial. While waiting the action of the grand jury, I broke jail and escaped and fled to Mexico. I just couldn't bear the thought of being separated from my daughter for so long a time. I had seen little enough of her during recent years as it was. She was living with her dead mother's people in El Paso. My wife was a Texas girl of Irish extraction; Mary got her blue eyes from her. I took a chance and visited her and told her what had happened, and that I'd have to go into hiding. Nothing would do her but that she go with me. We worked together in places in New Mexico and Arizona; I dealt cards and she danced. A rough life, but she liked it, and we were together. Finally we drifted back toward Texas.

"I'd heard of the gold strike here. A mining strike town is always a good place to hide. I grew a beard and changed my manner of dress. My hair was already turning grey. I had saved some money, and when I learned the Occidental was for sale, I bought it, hoping to prosper. I've been doing that, but Jess Rader recognised me; he was tending bar where I had my trouble and I think the man I killed was a friend of his."

"Don't doubt it," growled Lane. "And now I *know* the hellion had a killing coming. Go on."

"Rader threatened to expose me if I didn't work with him," Day resumed. "When he brought Richardson the gunman here to kill you, he insisted that I allow the killing to take place in my establishment. I pretended to agree, hoping I might find a way to help you if trouble started."

"You sure found a way, all right," Lane chuckled. His eyes were sparkling with excitement, for he had suddenly seen a great light.

"So Rader turned you in, eh?" he observed.

"That's right," said Day. "He said he was going to write a letter to the authorities telling them where to find me; I suppose he did. Perhaps it's for the best. I'm tired of hiding and running away."

Mort Lane managed to keep his face sober, although his eyes were dancing.

"And where did Rader write the letter to?" he asked casually, certain what the answer would be.

"To McMullen County. Lane, don't *you* recognise me now, despite the beard and the grey that wasn't in my hair when you met me five years ago?"

Lane still managed to keep his face straight. "Just what is your name?" he asked gravely. "I mean your real one?"

"Miguel de Alba," the other replied. "You see, in Spanish, Alba means dawn, daybreak. It loosely translates into Day, and of course Miguel is Michael. So I called myself Mike Day. Now do you remember?"

Mort Lane could hold in no longer. He seized Mike by the shoulders and shook him vigorously.

"You darned old horntoad!" he whooped.

"We've been hunting all over this end of creation for you, and all the time you were right under our noses! If this don't take the shingles off the barn! Mike, read this!"

He fished a crumpled letter from his pocket and thrust it into the other's hand. Mike de Alba, his eyes widening with incredulous unbelief, read the laconic response of the McMullen County authorities.

"Lane," he said, his voice quivering with emotion, "I can't believe it!"

"Maybe you can't, but just the same it's so," Lane chuckled. "There's nobody looking for you. And by the way, I've a notion you don't exactly care for the saloon business. Right?"

"Yes, you're right," Mike admitted. "But it and gambling are about all I know, and gambling is an uncertain way to make a living, to say the least."

"Well, you don't have to depend on either one for a living any longer," Lane said. He briefly explained the filing of the claim in the name of Pedro Lopez.

"And the way the money's piling up, Judge Arbaugh, the trustee, is raising Cain about the responsibility," he concluded. "I'll write to the Judge and arrange an appointment with him for next week. Then we'll ride down to Buckley and sign the necessary papers and you can take over your holdings."

Mike de Alba shook his head in bewilderment. "Things are coming too fast," he declared. "I suppose after a while I'll wake up and find I've been dreaming."

"You'll find it's an awfully lively dream," Lane chuckled. "And now let's get to something important. Is it all right for Mary and me to get married?"

Mike's smile was a bit tremulous when he replied, "Well, if she is willing, I certainly have no objection. I'll go over to the cabin and tell her you're here."

Lane's face was suddenly bleak. "I got a little chore to attend to, but I'll be back in an hour," he said. He hurried out, mounted Rojo and sent him up the trail to the mesa at a fast pace. He drew rein at The Mother Lode and entered.

Mayor Haskins was puttering around the bar. Lane took his marshal's badge from his pocket and dropped it before him.

"Bert," he said, "I'm resigning."

"What the devil!" sputtered the astonished mayor.

"Oh, I'll take it on again later, if you insist," Lane explained. "But right now I don't want the job; it'll sort of cramp my style."

He was out of the saloon and forking Rojo before the dazed Haskins could frame a reply.

Lane rode straight to the First Chance. He dismounted, entered the place and confronted the saloon-keeper.

"Rader," he said, "you're finished. Your little scheme to have Jack Richardson kill me backfired. I'm not here as a peace officer — I chucked the job a little while ago — and I'm not here as the owner of the property on which your business stands. I'm here as man to man to tell you to get out of town. I'm giving you one week to close up your affairs and vamoose. After the week's up, if you're still here, I'll kill you. This is Wednesday, I believe. Rader, next Wednesday, don't let the sun go down on you in Grave Town!"

Jess Rader went white. He quailed before the cold fury in Lane's eyes.

"I'll get out," he said thickly.

"See that you do," Lane told him, and left.

Lane wasted no time getting to the Occidental. He found Mary sitting at the table. Nobody else but the bartender was around. Her face was radiant with happiness; she seized his hand in both of hers and held on as if she never meant to let go.

"It's all so wonderful," she said, her voice

choking, "I can hardly believe it."

"Well, it's all true and we're all set," Lane replied. "Nothing more to worry about. That is, if you're still sure you want me."

"I wanted you the minute I first laid eyes on you," she declared. "And now you'll understand the real motive back of my little subterfuge. I knew about Dad's trouble of course, and how he felt about it, and even in the beginning, my dear, it would have been hard to say no to you. So when you jumped to your absurd conclusion about Dad and me, thinking I was his *criada*, his sweetheart, as they say in *Mejico*, I saw a chance to gain a little time in the hope that something might happen to make things better."

"Well, it happened, all right," Lane returned cheerfully. "And, honey, I got a notion: suppose we ride across to the Running W ranch-house and sort of look things over. We're going to live there, you know. There's nobody around, but I got the keys. What do you think?"

It was late when they rode back to the Occidental under the watching stars and through a world all glorious with moonlight.

"Well, what do you think, honey?" Lane said banteringly as they drew near the town.

"Had we better ride up to the mesa right away and see the new church and the preacher?"

Mary moved her horse in close to his, leaned over and kissed him. "Oh, I reckon *he* can wait till tomorrow," she said, with an undignified giggle.

CHAPTER XX

Jess Rader didn't take a week to get out of town. He was gone within three days.

"But I'll bet my interest in the blind lead that you haven't seen the last of him," Andy Webb declared pessimistically. "If I ever saw frozen murder it was in his face. You want to keep your eyes open for that sidewinder, Mort; he'll be out to even up the score. Yes, I'll bet you haven't seen the last of him."

Webb was right.

Mike de Alba didn't waste any time getting out of the saloon business. He sold the Occidental to his head bartender, payment to be made from the profits of the establishment.

"And now you can lend us a hand with the mines," Lane said. "There's plenty to keep all three of us busy. And I got another good notion for you."

"What's that?" asked Mike.

"Shave off those darn whiskers; they

make you look ten years older than you are."

"I will," Mike promised, and he did.

The following week Lane and his father-in-law headed for Buckley to keep their appointment with Judge Arbaugh.

"*Vaya usted con Dios!*" Mary told them, her eyes bright with happiness, voicing the old, old benediction with which the people of *Mejico* speed the well loved traveller on his way — *Vaya usted con Dios:* Go you with God!

The ride to Buckley was a long one, so they spent the night at Val Jackson's Cross C ranch-house, which was about half-way between Grave Town and Buckley.

"Us fellers will be working our south-west pasture tomorrow afternoon," Jackson told them when they were ready to continue their journey the following morning. "We'll keep an eye open for you and we'll ride back to the *casa* together. I want a chance to even up for that big jackpot Mike bluffed me out of with a busted flush. Uh-huh, we'll have another game tomorrow night, and I aims to set down poor and rise up rich!"

It was late afternoon when Lane and Mike reached Buckley. They quickly transacted their business with Judge Arbaugh, who voiced profane relief at being through with his responsibility. Then they dropped in on

Sheriff McDonald. He chuckled with pleasure when Lane told him the story of Pedro Lopez, the claim staked in his name and the vicissitudes Mike had undergone.

"Running away never gets a feller anything," he declared. "Better to look trouble in the eye and get it over with. Mort, I had that talk with the commissioners, and they authorised me to appoint you a deputy sheriff up at Grave Town. Here's your badge."

"Okay," Lane agreed, "but I doubt if I'll need it. Grave Town is so peaceful and quiet you can hear a pin drop."

The sheriff did not look convinced. "Uh-huh, a coupling pin on a tin roof, maybe. By the way, your friend Jess Rader is in town. No, I don't think he aims to coil his twine here. Heading for Arizona, I was told."

Lane and Mike spent the night in the cow town. They kept a sharp eye open for Jess Rader, but didn't see him. Which was not strange. Rader saw them ride into Buckley and shortly afterward he rode *out* of town, heading north on the Buckley Trail.

The following morning they set out on their return trip. About mid-afternoon they were drawing near the south line of the Cross C holdings. The trail ran through a belt of heavily wooded hills, their dark slopes slashed by occasional narrow and gloomy canyons. A few miles farther on, the hills petered out and the rangeland began — John Bruton's holdings to the east and Val Jackson's to the west of the trail.

They were passing beneath the wide-spreading branches of a great tree when Lane glanced up at a slight sound of rustling in the leaves over their heads — glanced up just an instant too late. Two ropes snaked down from amid the foliage. Close loops settled over their shoulders and were instantly jerked tight, wrenching them from their saddles to strike the ground with stunning force. Before they could make a move, forms dashed out of the encroaching growth and hard, sinewy bodies were all over them. Their arms were pinned to their sides by turn on turn of the ropes, the knots made fast. Then, still dazed by the fall, they were lifted back to their saddles and their ankles securely bound to the stirrup straps. Their guns were plucked from their holsters.

A cold chill went over Mort Lane as he gazed on the dark, savage faces of their captors.

"Renegade Mescalero Apache breeds!" he muttered to his fellow captive. "Mike, we're in a bad spot, and it's all my fault. I should have remembered that these people have long memories for blood feuds and will wait for a chance to even the score for years. I should have always been on my guard. I expect those five Andy Webb and I killed that first night on the mesa belonged to the same tribe. I reported the killings to the Indian agent, of course, and I reckon the word got back to their folks. They've just been biding their time and waiting for a chance at me. But it's a shame I had to drag you into it with me!"

"Never mind about that," said Mike. "Where do you suppose they're taking us?"

"To their encampment back in the hills somewhere, I reckon," Lane replied. "We'll be mighty lucky if we don't end up the main event of a barbecue party."

However, Mort Lane was wrong in his guess. Soon the breeds turned into a narrow canyon which they followed for some miles, finally coming to a halt in front of an old but tightly built cabin almost hidden by the encroaching growth. It was doubtless the former home of some prospector or trapper. Here the captives were dismounted and, their arms still bound to their sides — their discomfort meant nothing to the breeds — were herded into the cabin, which consisted of two rooms. They were hustled across to the inner room, a door was slammed shut and a bolt shot. They could hear the Apaches talking in gutteral tones in the outer room.

"Mike, there's something queer about this," Lane said. "Apaches don't live in this kind of a place. Why the devil did they bring us here? I can't figure it."

De Alba held up his hand for silence. "I can understand something of their talk," he whispered. "Let me listen."

As he listened, his face grew puzzled. Finally, when the outer door had opened and slammed shut again, he turned to Lane and said in low tones:

"I couldn't catch all that was said, but I gather they were paid to capture us and bring us here. They're holding us for somebody. One remains to keep a watch on us. The others rode to fetch whoever it is they're holding us for. I gather they won't be gone long."

Lane whistled under his breath. "Left one man to guard us, eh?" he whispered. "If it wasn't for these ropes! With my hands loose, I could bust that door down with my shoulder, easy. Chances are he'd do for us both, but that would be better than the stake or a slow fire, or whatever it is they've got in store for us."

"Lane, if you can knock that door down, I

205

believe we have a chance," Mike whispered back. "My hands are very slender, a dealer's hands, and my wrists are supple. I managed to steal a little space while they were tying me, without them catching on. If you can just loosen the knots a little with your teeth, I believe I can get my hands free. No, no, you can't chew a hair rope — you should know that — but you may be able to loosen the knots."

His heart beating fast with revived hope, Lane went to work on the knots. Due to Mike's clever subterfuge, the rope was already loose about his flexible wrists.

But it was a terrific task he had set himself. A hair rope ties a stubborn knot and its hard, smooth surface is like that of a steel cable. And to make matters worse, Lane knew he was working against time. At any moment the rest of the bunch might return. His mouth was bleeding, his gums torn and raw when he felt a knot loosen a little. Five more minutes of frenzied effort and Mike was able to slip the strands up to his elbows. His deft fingers quickly undid the knots that held his companion. Another moment and both were free.

Rubbing the circulation back into their numbed arms, they listened intently and could hear the breed moving about in the other room. He was undoubtedly very much on the alert.

"If we only had a gun!" Lane breathed. "I can knock the door down with one rush."

"We have one!" Mike whispered back. "These people never heard of a sleeve holster. I have a little double-barrelled derringer — my 'gambler's gun' — in my sleeve. It's second nature with a dealer always to pack the darned thing. They didn't find it when they searched us for weapons."

"Then it's a cinch!" Lane breathed exultantly as Mike slid the stubby little iron into his palm. "I'll hit the door with everything I've got and slew sideways along the wall. You let him have it the second the door goes down. He won't be able to get more than one of us, that's sure."

"And if so, that one will be you," Mike said. "There's no other way; I'm not strong enough to knock down the door. But if you die," he added grimly, "you'll not die alone."

They paused to listen again. A smell of wood smoke was drifting through the cracks in the door. They could hear steps moving about and the clatter of pots and pans. Evidently the guard had started a fire in the stove and was preparing a meal. That was all to the good. He might have his hands full at the moment they broke out. Lane motioned Mike to take up his post beside the door. Then he backed against the far wall, drew a deep breath and gathered his strength. He didn't expect to be alive five seconds later. He dashed across the room at a dead run, and hurled his two hundred pounds against the door.

There was a crash of splintering wood, a screech of disrupted metal. The door flew open, sagging crazily on one hinge. Lane charged into the room.

The breed was standing by the stove. He whirled around, hand streaking to his holster. The cabin rocked to a double report.

CHAPTER XXI

Mort Lane felt the wind of the passing bullet. Then he saw the breed go down, thrashing and clawing, as the second barrel of Mike's derringer let go. He was dead when Lane reached him, fist poised to strike.

Lane swept the cabin with a swift glance. "There are our guns on the table!" he exclaimed. He made a dive for his Colts and holstered them.

"Now if they just didn't take our horses with them!" he hoped. "And I don't think they did. I didn't hear any irons on the rocks when they rode away; just the thud of unshod hooves. Come on, Mike; let's look. We've got to get out of here in a hurry, anyhow."

They left the cabin, glancing around, ready for instant action. There was nobody in sight.

"There are our horses under a lean-to, with the rigs still on them," Mike exclaimed exultantly. "Now what shall we do?"

"Strike it down the canyon and hope we get out before they come back," Lane instantly decided. "Can't risk going up it — it may be a box, and then they'll have us cornered. We may meet them coming back, but we'll have to chance it. Maybe we won't; they've been gone only a little over an hour. All depends on how far they had to go to notify whoever it was they did the chore for."

They forked the horses and turned them down the canyon. "It's already getting gloomy in this crack," Lane observed hopefully. "That will be in our favour if we do run into a shindig. Sift sand! That roan of yours looks like he can get up and go, and I'll hold Rojo in if necessary. If we can just make it outside to the trail, we'll be okay."

Down the darkening canyon they sped, as fast as the rough and broken ground would permit. Lane strained his ears anxiously to catch the first sound of approaching horses, but as the miles rolled past under their clicking irons his spirits rose.

"I believe we're going to make it," he told Mike. "Can't be more than another mile to the canyon mouth, and it's getting darker by the minute."

A stretch strewn with loose boulders and

choked with brush forced them to slow down, and Lane grew anxious again. Then abruptly he uttered a jubilant exclamation. Directly ahead the canyon broadened and brightened; its mouth and the open range lay before them.

A moment more and they dashed from the gorge and swerved into the northbound trail. But just as they reached it, a band of seven horsemen bulged around a bend to the south and not three hundred yards distant. Six of the riders were Apache breeds. The seventh was a tall, lean white man whom Lane instantly recognised.

"Jess Rader!" he shouted. "I might have known it! They were holding us for Rader! Ride, Mike, ride! If that son of Satan gets his hands on us we're done for!"

A storm of yells arose as Rader and the breeds sighted them, then a roar of gunfire. Bullets whistled past or kicked up spurts of dust. Mike's roan gave a convulsive bound and sped up the trail in an astonishing burst of speed. Bending low in the saddle, Lane sent Rojo charging after him. The red sorrel snorted his indignation at being distanced and set about overtaking the roan without delay. He slugged his head above the bit, his steely legs drove backwards like pistons, and he fairly poured his long body over the ground.

Mort Lane glanced back over his shoulder. Lead was still whistling past altogether too close for comfort, but the pursuit was dropping back. Their horses were no match for Rojo, and Mike's roan was giving an excellent account of himself.

"I'd like to stop and settle accounts with you, *Señor* Rader," Lane muttered, "but I guess I'd better not. That is, unless you're loco enough to pull ahead of your bunch. Reckon you've got too much savvy for that, though."

Rojo was quickly overhauling the speeding roan — too quickly, Lane suddenly realised; Mike's horse was faltering. Another moment and they were shoulder to shoulder.

"What's the matter, Mike?" Lane called anxiously, tightening his grip on Rojo's bridle and slowing him so the other could keep pace.

"They got my horse," de Alba replied. "He's hit bad. He'll go down in a minute; already floundering."

Breathing an oath, Lane pulled Rojo in still more. Behind them the yells were growing louder, and the slugs were coming closer. He held Rojo abreast of the lagging roan.

"Quick! Flop on behind me!" he told Mike. "Hustle!"

"Go on!" Mike jolted back. "He can't carry the double weight. Go on and save yourself. Mary is waiting for you."

"Up behind me!" Lane roared again. "Do you want us both to stop here and get killed? Rojo can pack us. We'll see this through together or not at all."

Mike obeyed the order, and barely had he backed the sorrel behind Lane when the roan gave a choking scream, faltered in his stride and fell, to lie in a quivering heap.

And now what had been an exhilarating chase changed to a grim race with death. Rojo gallantly gave his best, but the pursuers slowly closed in on the overburdened horse. Bullets began coming close.

Mort Lane glanced back, his face set in bleak lines. Now less than two hundred yards separated them from the exultant pursuers.

"We can't do it," he told his companion. "We'll go through that thicket ahead, unfork and shoot it out with them. Anyhow, I aim to take Jess Rader with me when I go."

They crashed through the thicket, the trail curving sharply and giving them a moment's surcease from the storm of lead. They bulged out the far side of the thicket.

Lane loosened his feet in the stirrups and pulled Rojo to a halt.

"Look!" Mike suddenly yelled. "Coming this way!"

Galloping across the prairie toward them were nearly a dozen horsemen.

"It's Val Jackson and his bunch!" shouted Lane. "They said they'd be down this way on the lookout for us. They must have heard the shooting. Hi, Val, come a-running and lend a hand! We're in a spot!"

Whooping excitedly, the Cross C bunch charged up to the trail just as Jess Rader and his breeds burst from the thicket to be met by a hail of bullets. Down went the dark-faced riders as Jackson and his men grimly closed in, guns blazing.

"Rader's getting away!" shouted Mike.

The lean killer had whirled his big bay and was speeding back the way he had come. Even as Mike spoke the thicket swallowed him and he vanished from sight.

"Unfork!" Lane cried. "I'll get him!"

Mike leaped to the ground. Lane whirled Rojo and sent him flashing in pursuit of Rader. With yells and curses the Cross C riders followed, but were quickly outdistanced by the flying sorrel. Lane settled himself in the saddle and called on Rojo to do his darnedest.

Rojo responded nobly. He snorted, rolled his eyes and hurled himself after the straining bay.

Rader was well mounted, but the bay was no match for the great sorrel. Steadily Rojo closed the distance. They reached the canyon mouth, Rader shooting over his shoulder. Lane heard the whine of the passing slugs but grimly held his own fire and gave his whole attention to riding. Rader swerved his horse and darted into the canyon with Rojo less than a score of yards behind.

Suddenly Rader gave up. He jerked the bay to a sliding halt, whirled him about and faced his pursuer, gun flaming. Lane dropped the split reins to the ground, whipped out his Colts and answered Rader shot for shot.

It was almost dark in the canyon; the guns spurted reddish fire. The gorge roared and echoed to the reports as the maddened horses plunged and reared. Their riders were shadowy, weaving wraiths blasting death at one another through the gloom.

Mort Lane felt the burn of a bullet searing his ribs. Another stung the flesh of his cheek. A third turned his hat sideways on his head.

Then suddenly Jess Rader screamed a

high-pitched scream of agony and terror. He reeled in his saddle, tried with a straining hand to raise his gun for one last shot, and could not. He plunged sideways and thudded to the ground.

Lane dismounted stiffly and walked toward where Rader lay. Abruptly he was very, very tired. He was gazing down at the dead man when the Cross C riders came thundering into the canyon.

"You all right, Mort?" Val Jackson called anxiously. "You got blood on your face."

"Just a scratch," Lane told him. "Yes, everything's in hand."

Suddenly a thought struck him. He fumbled in his pocket and drew forth the deputy sheriff's badge Sheriff McDonald had given him. He glanced at it disgustedly.

"Plumb forgot I had it," he said. "A fine law enforcement officer I am! A good peace officer brings in his man instead of plugging him full of holes!"

Val Jackson bellowed with laughter. "Well," he chuckled, "I reckon Rader was killed resisting arrest; we'll all swear to it. Don't matter anyhow, just so long as he's dead. Catch his horse, somebody, and Mike can ride it. We'll leave Rader for the sheriff, if the buzzards don't get him first and pizen themselves. And now let's get going; enough of this foolishness. It's getting late and we've got something important on hand. We got a poker game set for tonight. Let's go!"

The poker game lasted till the wee small hours, and it was around noon the following day before Lane and Mike were ready for the trail.

"I'm riding with you," Val Jackson decided. "And you work dodgers might as well come along, too," he told his hands. "I won ten bucks last night and feel like celebrating."

"That ten will cost him fifty before the night's over," one of the cowboys chuckled to Lane. "He's always like that when he wins a few pesos."

The lovely blue dusk was sifting down from the hilltops and the stars were coming out when they sighted, in the distance, what appeared to be a cluster of fallen stars but was in reality the golden lights of Grave Town. Val Jackson eyed them with appreciation.

"Sure looks purty," he observed. "And just a while back there wasn't anything there but yippin' coyotes. Mort, no matter what else you did or didn't do, you built a town!"

As they drew near the glowing lights, a mellow clanging sounded on the still air.

"Now what?" wondered Jackson. "Do they have church every night up there?"

"That isn't the church bell," Lane answered. "It must be the new school bell they're trying out. I heard they figured to hang it today."

"Sounds nice," said Jackson. "I always liked schools — so long as I didn't have to be inside 'em."

Lane was silent for a while; then suddenly he laughed aloud.

"Now what's so darned funny?" Jackson demanded.

"I was just thinking," Lane replied. "I sure didn't figure on it when Andy Webb was planning to build it, but that school is going to come in handy, in a few years, for Mary and me."

We hope you have enjoyed this Large Print Edition. Other Thorndike, Wheeler or Chivers Press Large Print books are available at your library or directly from the publishers.

For more information about current and upcoming titles, please call or write, without obligation, to:

Publisher
Thorndike Press
295 Kennedy Memorial Drive
Waterville, ME 04901
Tel. (800) 223-1244

Or visit our Web site at:
www.gale.com/thorndike
www.gale.com/wheeler

OR

Chivers Large Print
published by BBC Audiobooks Ltd
St James House, The Square
Lower Bristol Road
Bath BA2 3SB
England
Tel. +44(0) 800 136919
email: bbcaudiobooks@bbc.co.uk
www.bbcaudiobooks.co.uk

All our Large Print titles are designed for easy reading, and all our books are made to last.